Breaking the Habit

The White Lie

Niall Conway

978-1-917728-11-9
©Niall Conway 2025

Orla Kelly Publishing,
27 Kilbrody,
Mount Oval,
Rochestown,
Cork,
Ireland.

A £1 contribution from the sale of each book will go towards Foyle Hospice in Derry. Please support this worthy charitable cause.

Contents

In memory of Jane Bernadette.

I would like to sincerely thank my sister Nuala (Bradley) who is always my first point of contact for feedback and not forgetting her husband Damien who both provide excellent-constructive critique on my latest writing project.

I would also like to thank Orla Kelly of Orla Kelly Publishing for her patience and all-round expertise in all aspects of publishing this book.

Chapter 1

Free

6th October 2011

As she closed the door and put the letter through the letterbox, it was finally over. Her heart was pounding like never before: frenetic, frantic, furious. The seconds and minutes right up to this had passed by in a contorted haze of doubt, fear and no little adrenaline. In the hours before, she couldn't speak to a single person in any coherent fashion. After breakfast that morning, she had excused herself from lunch to begin the final packing and, more importantly, imbue herself with the mental fortitude to make her break.

Sarah had written the letter the night before in an emotional surge where the last two years of her life flashed before her. Something she thought would take a few minutes took nearly two hours. At school, competency in English and all things writing was never a problem, but for these minutes, she encountered a mental block for the first time. How can you put two-plus years into a couple of pages, she thought to herself. How can you try to explain to the hierarchy? Would they understand? Would they want to understand? And maybe, just maybe, the key to all of this might be that they actually might agree with Sarah's decision. This is why she felt she had to leave without a discussion or, more likely, another confrontation.

The letter was now complete. She couldn't believe what a struggle this was, yet paradoxically, it proved somewhat cathartic and gave her the inner strength for the following evening. Sleep was never going to be easy on a night like this. After the letter was finished, she read, hoping this might make her drowsy. It partially worked as she nodded off at about 1 a.m. on top of her bed. When she awoke a few minutes later, she switched off the light and climbed into bed. Not surprisingly, as she feared, it wasn't a great night's sleep, but she was thankful it would be her last there, a fact only she and her cousin Rosie, back home, knew of. This, for Sarah, was the biggest regret of all, the fact she couldn't bear to tell her two best friends in the convent.

The next day she showed up for breakfast on time as always and politely made conversation with the handful of others who regularly shared her breakfast slot. She used this opportunity to discretely make her excuse for lunch to one of her friends. It wasn't as if she didn't have friends there; she had. Sarah was very popular, particularly among the younger element. She could honestly say she had made two firm friendships that she hoped she could reignite someday, but not for a while yet. She felt guilty that she couldn't or wouldn't tell them about her plans. It wasn't as if she couldn't trust them not to tell 'the mob'; instead, Sarah felt it would be a quicker, more seamless exit if no one on the inside knew. She laughed at the thought of her two pals' reaction to the senior sisters finding out. Her two pals were 'Sister Colette' and 'Sister Angela'. In a day of taut emotion, this brought a wry and unfamiliar smile to Sarah's demure face. With lunch excused, it was time for her afternoon chores and the obligatory spiritual matters. This she found a lot easier than expected. To her friends, whom she hoped she would see again, she was even more welcoming than usual and took great solace in trying to help them out as much as possible. This was her way of saying her thanks and goodbyes all in one. If only they knew.

***

She faintly heard the letter hit the reception floor. It wasn't exactly a dramatic exit but rather a surreptitious yet brisk walk through the gates for the last time. For fear of someone seeing her even though she wanted to, she dared not look back, not even in anger. She waited until she was outside the gates and another thirty metres down the road before she glanced back briefly. Her heart was still racing as she made her way to the high street, a ten-minute walk from the convent. Then, and only then, could she relax.

It was approaching 7 p.m. on a dry but cold October evening, with dusk as ever winning its battle with the lingering light of the day. She entered the nearest café and waited in line to be served. It housed a small eating area with traditional square tables and red and yellow chequered tablecloths, not that Sarah noticed such detail.

'What you want, dahlin?' a local girl with a chirpy cockney accent asked. Sarah stared at the lady behind the counter, but her brain was not in gear.

- What you want dahlin?' the lady asked again,
- 'I.., I.., I don't know, I'm not sure', Sarah replied in a still flustered state.
- 'Well, I hope it's not a haircut cos they're next door', the lady replied swiftly, followed by a hearty chuckle to herself.

'C'mon, luv what is it?'…you're keeping everyone else waiting.' Before another chuckle, Sarah said sorry and turned around to see no one behind her.
- 'I'm only joking, dahlin….there's no-one behind ya… you must be working too many hours luv….you wanna get a handy number like this'.

'Just a tea and a wee muffin, please', Sarah responded.

'No bother, sweetheart. Have a seat, and I'll bring it down.' Sarah sat down.

Her head was still in another place. Where this place was exactly, she didn't know. This, her first social interaction liberated from her 'habit', hadn't gone well. She hoped it wouldn't be a sign of things to come. She needed a friend… Ten Silk Cut would be the answer for now. She returned to the lady behind the counter and asked for cigarettes, this time without the drama. Sitting down again, she lit her cigarette, the first one since she was at her cousin's wedding in Ballymena in August. That day, she had only smoked three, four in total, but she did enjoy the occasional cigarette when she got a chance. Her first inhalation was a bit clumsy. The second was different, as soon as she exhaled, she slowly but surely saw the last couple of years ebb away in seconds as the truncated plume of smoke meandered its way across the café. With her daydream over, her brain was now awakened from its temporary slumber. She sat up straight in her chair, and she felt awake and alive. She finished her first cup of tea and had another one and another cigarette. The beauty of the moment was the simplicity of the moment. Emancipated!

Was this the moment Sarah had waited for the last few months? Was her nightmare finally over? The tsunami of turmoil rebounding in her head seemed to be clearing, for now anyway.

Refreshed and reinvigorated she made her way into the town centre with a now more purposeful stride. Sarah was on a mission, a destination somewhere, anywhere but here. Her cousin Rosie even though a student had sent over some money that was to take care of Sarah for a couple of weeks. She would pay this back in due course, but as ever with Rosie, this wasn't at her insistence but Sarah's. Not surprisingly, although a bit nervous she felt good as she made her way to the small hotel she had decided to stay in for the night. She had only ever stayed in a hotel three, possibly four times previously, when she was in her teens. Both occasions were with her family. Mum, Dad, and older sister Mairead. The occasions were weekend breaks in Galway; her father was not really one for sun holidays. This would be different, though, as she was now in charge of her own affairs. She made her way to reception and duly asked if there were any rooms left.

-'No problem, madam, one night or two' was the reply from someone with an accent. The young, pleasant girl was from either Australia or New Zealand, which one she wasn't sure, but she wasn't from around these parts.

-'Oh, just the one', said Sarah.

-'How do you intend to pay, madam, by credit card, visa?' was the next question.

-'Is cash ok?' Sarah asked nervously.

-'Cash madam, cash will be fine'.

-'We'll need a deposit of £40.00 though, is that ok?'

-'Why, how much is it altogether?', Sarah then asked hurriedly

-'£80.00 in total, madam.'

A bit startled and surprised by the price, Sarah confirmed, 'It's okay…I'll give you the lot now'.

'No problem, madam. Here's your card. Just take the lift to the second floor, and it's on your left. Breakfast is served between seven and nine. Have a nice stay.'

Although not the 'Ritz', Sarah was taken aback not only by the price but how the hotel key was a plastic card.

Her exuberance and excitement of a few minutes before had now gone. She began to doubt herself again…. was she prepared for life on the outside? She moved swiftly away from reception and the pristine uniform of the receptionist. She was simply too embarrassed to ask how the damn thing worked. She went to the second floor with her trolley bag behind her. Her worldly possessions in one solitary bag. She stared at the card, 'what way does this work?'…she thought. She saw an arrow sign and tried it. Like all other 'card rookies', she made the inevitable mistake of keeping the card in too long. But Sarah was no slouch and, in a few seconds, had sussed it. Maybe this 'going straight' would be handy enough after all. She placed her bag on the floor and plumped herself on the bed. She looked around her room and couldn't believe how large it was. It even had a double bed. The bathroom had fresh towels and a brand-new colour TV in the main room. Maybe it *was* worth the eighty quid. While in the convent, watching TV was confined to a couple of hours each evening and a Saturday night, so she was drawn between watching TV or heading 'out on the town'. Her 'out on the town' certainly wouldn't be clubbing but possibly going to a pub in the high street and having a drink or two. The thought of sitting in a bar, not worrying about who would be watching or what time it was, was so appealing she went for the latter.

For a few minutes, though, she sat back on the bed and switched the TV on. The bed was massive; unlike the confined spaces of her 'cell' back at the convent, she wasn't used to this. She smiled as she lay there watching one of the many meaningless soap operas to choose from. Had they found the letter yet? No, it was probably too early.

Chapter 2

A Big Night Out

By now, it was 8.40 p.m. She would make her way into town. She decided not to dress up as such. Her civvy uniform would do as is. She grabbed her small handbag and made for the door. She stopped in her tracks to comb her hair. Suddenly, unexpectedly, she felt naked. She had no make-up and wasn't wearing accessories of any kind. She was allowed these in moderation in her convent days for her civic duties but had left what little she had behind there as her one suitcase could only hold so much. Undeterred, she set off; it wasn't as if she was going to meet someone, a 'Mr Right' tonight; the thought of meeting someone, a relationship even, was for the future but definitely not tonight.

Sarah made her way into town and decided to go into 'The Wellington' one of the busier pubs on the high street, given that it was a Thursday night. She went to the bar and ordered a 'West Coast Cooler', thinking she might venture to a beer or cider next time. As she waited for her drink, she began to feel a bit strange. Here she was, in a bar on her own on a weeknight. The strangeness turned into mild paranoia, and Sarah felt everyone staring at her. She couldn't wait to get her drink and sit in a quiet corner of the bar. Sarah, for obvious reasons, wasn't a big drinker and most definitely not used to having 'a swift half' on a weeknight. When she sat down, she spied a paper and grabbed it, pretending to read; soon, her flustered state quickly evaporated, and she began to feel relaxed, slowly taking in the other punters inside. It would be one of the many moments in her transformation to 'normalisation'.

Her very first taste of alcohol was the night of her seventeenth birthday when she drank a couple of bottles of beer but didn't really enjoy the taste. It was a month later before she would try again, and since then, she had flirted intermittently between the odd bottle of Budweiser and cider. A disciplined and diligent student, Sarah didn't socialise an awful lot in those days but liked getting out occasionally to unwind from the pressure of her studies. Initially, on starting her A-levels, she thought she would follow in the footsteps of her older sister, who had just started Teacher Training College in Belfast. This, she thought about, seemed a very natural and logical choice. She needed three Bs in her A-levels, and her projected grades at the end of her first A-level year seemed promising. Tonight though, she was a world away from all of that. After her first sip, she went for her Silk Cut again. Although enjoying her nicotine fix, she decided that when this packet was finished, she wouldn't buy any more, or so she thought anyway. But for the moment, especially when she was having a drink, the two would be inextricably linked. She surveyed the surroundings. There was a decent mix of punters inside. From a few businessmen still in their suits to a few happy couples to groups of younger people helping to increase the decibel levels. This felt good. Had she made the right decision? Oh yes. This very ordinary yet exciting scene after a momentary anxious blip had proved it, no doubt.

She thought to herself inquisitively, 'I wonder where I'll be in twelve months?' Time would tell.

Had they read the letter now, she wondered? If only she and her fellow sisters had the luxury of a mobile phone, she could call or text her friends in the convent to hear the gossip. However, such luxuries were not bestowed upon the sisters. Now suitably relaxed, she began reminiscing about her time in the convent.

Her first year was blissful. Possibly an over-extended honeymoon period, but she enjoyed it. Freed from the intense pressure of A-Levels, she enjoyed the whole regime of early morning prayers; breakfast, work duties, lunch, more chores, evening meal, prayers, watching some TV, and bed. Repetitive and orderly it may have been, but Sarah soon settled into the convent. Although quiet by nature, she was sociable and quickly made friends with all those inside, especially the younger element who were inquisitive of the new girl and what she would bring to the convent. She even found Mother Superior very welcoming and approachable. She went out of her way to stress that Sarah was an important fixture in the convent and would soon give her appropriate duties. After a later one-to-one chat with the Mother Superior, or 'the soup' as some called her, Sarah would have two main dedicated jobs. In the morning, she would work on the convent accounts. At that time, all the accounts were prepared and recorded manually, a very antiquated system, if truth be told. She was to take this job over from one of the elder stateswomen in the convent, Sister Benedict. Sarah's first job would be to use her IT skills to track and monitor all spending electronically.

Although Sarah wasn't a whiz on the computer, she didn't want to, nor couldn't say no, so she agreed to do her morning chores. Her second chore which she was to spend from 2.00 to 5.30 p.m. doing, was again IT related. She was to open all mail received in the morning post and reply to all formal or informal communications. The Mother Superior would have to oversee and sign off on all formal letters, but Sarah would type up all first drafts at the very least. This, she was a lot more comfortable with. As Sarah had 'A-Level' English, typing up letters was something she was looking forward to. This aspect of her chores she settled into very quickly and made an early, positive impression, especially on 'the soup'. Her competence, even flair for writing, had eased the burden on the Mother Superior, thus making Sarah the flavour of the month. The accounts side of things took a bit longer for Sarah to get on top of, but portraying the commitment she had in successfully passing three A-Levels the year before meant it wasn't too long before she had the accounts displayed in a user-friendly and highly transparent fashion. To say the least, she felt this was very much in spite of rather than because of her 'accounts mentor' Sister Benedict. Sarah felt 'Bendy' as she was sometimes called had not been as cooperative with the handover as she could have been! On some occasions - Knowledge definitely is power.

Weekends were more relaxed; certainly, there was plenty of prayer time, especially on Sundays, but Saturdays were, in effect, your 'day off'. Well, in reality, it was every other day off, as on alternate Saturdays, you were expected to do some of your designated charity work or visit various hospitals, nursing homes or hostels in the locality. On the other Saturday afternoons, though, you were allowed to shop and meet up with friends in the morning and early afternoon as long as the curfew of 3 p.m. was adhered to. Often, Sarah and her two 'sister pals' would go into the local high street, sometimes in their civvies, drink tea and watch the world go by.

As time went on, Sarah became more and more organised and confident in her chores; she found neither overly demanding and was easily coping with the assigned workload. Sister Colette, one of her pals, after a few weeks then, relayed one of the best pieces of advice she received during her time there,

-'Sarah, whatever you do, don't ever say you're not busy or comfortable in your chores, otherwise you'll only end up getting more and something you probably won't like'. The message was received and very much understood. As time passed, Sarah even had time to revisit one of her favourite hobbies, painting. Having considered and often regretted not pursuing A-Level Art after excelling at GCSE level, Sarah, already an accomplished artist, spent some of her spare time painting, even getting some sold in the local Oxfam charity shop for a nominal fee. The monies she happily gave back to the Oxfam store and some other local charities. Other than painting, the only other hobby she could squeeze into her busy schedule was reading; Sarah was an avid reader from an early age and occasionally read to ease her to sleep. Happy in her chores, with a few new friends and, more importantly, happy in her increasing spirituality, Sarah was soon convinced she had made the right career choice.

Her vocation to the convent didn't come in a premonition or based on a defining life-threatening incident. Sarah was born into a typical Irish Catholic family in the small provincial town of Ballycastle in County Antrim, some fifty miles north of Belfast. Her mum was devout for sure and espoused all things religious, both spiritually and socially. Her dad, Fran, was a bit more 'lapsed' but did go to Mass every weekend. In fact, all the family went to church 'religiously' each weekend and holy days, with the sacraments, also mandatory in the Delargy household. Sarah had gone to the local Convent Grammar in the town like her sister before, ironically called 'Cross & Passion'. Her leaning towards religion and the convent was gradual. If there was a spark, it was possibly the passing away of her maternal grandmother. She lived a few doors away and had a profound and meaningful impact on all the Delargys, including Sarah. Sarah was fourteen at the time, and although sad at losing her grandmother, the abiding memory for her was the reaction of her mum. Her mum was devastated.

At the funeral, the sight of her inconsolable mother was permanently etched into the psyche of the youngest Delargy. Her mum had lost her inspiration, her soulmate. The pair were inseparable; the only saving grace for Anna, Sarah's mum, was that her mother's illness was short and relatively painless. This was the crux. Anna was sure her painless passing was due to divine inspiration. This left an indelible mark on an impressionable teenager. A seed was sown. Gradually, Sarah, more than her sister Mairead, began to embrace all things religious, especially in times of stress like exams, where she felt God would provide a helping hand through any adversity. This was only accentuated when Sarah received excellent GCSE results, passing all ten, eight of which were at Grade A.

When choosing A-Levels, Sarah chose French, English and History. She toyed with the idea of R.E. and Art. Indeed, one of her close friends, Clare Campbell, had tried to coax Sarah to join the Religion A-level class, but Sarah decided to stick with her original decision. During these couple of years, she became more contemplative and enjoyed her 'secret' visits to the local chapel. She found this calming for whatever reason and felt things were much clearer in her head after each visit. The initial impromptu visits were ones her mum didn't even know about. So much so that it was only at the end of her first A-level year that she eventually talked to her mum about the prospect of joining the Carmelite sisters in London. As ever, Sarah had confided in Rosie before speaking to her mum. Initially shocked, her mum eventually warmed to the idea and said, 'If it's meant to be, it's meant to be'. Her dad wasn't so comfortable with this at all. In fact, from the very day she announced this to her father, she felt a slight distance emerge between them, which hadn't been there before. He wasn't convinced about her career path. Was it he who had the real premonition?

Her dad was an electrician by trade and had his own business of sorts, employing four or five others as the business grew from strength to strength in recent years. He was very dark set, tall and moustached. He had also amassed a bit of a 'beer-belly', something Sarah believed he was secretly proud of. He enjoyed his few pints on a Saturday night in the local pub. A reformed heavy smoker's only current vice would be the odd visit to the bookies for a punt on a horse or two and the regular as-clockwork Saturday football bet. Football was his real passion and pastime. A lot of the weekend, he was transfixed on 'Sky Sports', a remote control glued to his left hand. He was an easy-going, affable character who enjoyed and revelled in all the 'craic' and slagging that came with *his* vocation, 'Manchester United Football Club'. He was heavily involved with the local football team in his spare time. Previously, he had coached the youth team before settling for an administrative role on the club committee. His wife reckoned he devoted too much time to this, but when Sarah's dad got involved in something, it was 'full duck or no dinner' as he would say himself. Fran Delargy doesn't do half-measures.

Some of these traits would prove to be genetic. Sarah was an attractive girl; at '5:6' she was tall and slim and, like her dad, had dark hair and a swarthy complexion, also dimpled, this time like her mum. Such a complexion was not the most prevalent human feature at the very top of the Island of Ireland. She was quiet and unassuming to most but did open up in the company of friends and was in her own laconic style, witty and charming when she wanted to be. With an innocent yet endearing smile, she enjoyed the odd giggle with her close friends. Throughout her schooldays, she maintained the same hairstyle, which was short and tidy, usually with a fringe. Although quiet, again like her dad, Sarah, if needed, wasn't afraid to fight her corner. Although shy, her mum always struggled with how Sarah was such an integral and successful member of the school debating team.

Her mum's interest in football was more passive, and not surprisingly, she was a quieter individual than her husband. She was of average height with shoulder-length auburn hair, and there were certainly a few extra pounds nowadays than visible on her wedding photograph, proudly displayed in the living room. She worked part-time as a classroom assistant in the local primary school, 'the best wee job in the world', she would often say.

What had gone so wrong then after year two for Sarah? Year two in the life of a nun was very important. Essentially, when first entering the convent, Sarah was to serve what, in practical terms, was a two-year apprenticeship called 'the novitiate'. It is only after these two years that she becomes a fully-fledged nun. As year two progressed, the first major inklings of doubt engulfed her mind. Initially, she put this down to a natural reaction and knew that this wasn't uncommon for all nuns. After speaking about it to Sister Angela and Sister Colette, this was her synopsis anyway. It was mid-way through year two that she seriously began to question her calling. She was still happy with life in general but was becoming increasingly frustrated by some of the higher committee's actions or, more accurately, non-actions.

The convent had a basic structure. There were four senior sisters, including the mother superior; the other nineteen were below this, all of equal standing. The higher committee had four very disparate characters. There were two in particular (Sister Benedict & Sister Ignatius) with whom Sarah found it difficult to develop any kind of rapport. Time after time at their monthly meetings, these two in particular would not only interrupt Sarah but more commonly shoot down her comments, ideas, or suggestions, irrespective of how practical or progressive they might have been. Such derision began to eat at Sarah. So much so that Sarah went to see the 'Mother Superior' after one particular meeting, wanting some answers. Sarah's sin on this occasion was to suggest preparing monthly accounts as opposed to 'quarterly formally', something Sarah felt would keep her organised and leave less work and stress for the quarterly and annual reports; after all, it was Sarah and Sarah alone who would have the extra work. However, as approachable as the Mother Superior was, Sarah wasn't impressed by her response…simply putting things down to a generation gap. Sarah, by now, felt exasperated and let down.

For a few weeks, she was in a chasm. She was trying to be proactive and improve things for everyone's benefit, yet the obstinance and intransigence of a couple of people were winning the day. She confided in Sister Angela.

-'Look, Sarah, don't beat yourself up about this; we have all been there before you. You're a good sister, and you bring way more to this place than you think; don't let it affect you or curb your enthusiasm. Look, you probably don't know this as yet, but it's Sister Benedict who runs this place, not the Mother Superior; no one ever questions or challenges her. Sarah, you know I'm a big believer in Karma; things will work out, trust me.

Sincere words, they were but scant consolation to a wounded soul. Not freefall exactly but things had irrevocably changed post this latest meeting. Sarah and Sister Angela often joked about the number of foreign holidays Bendy seemed to take and judging by her complexion on her return; she wasn't going to the north of Scotland, more likely jaunts to the Mediterranean or somewhere similar.

What was the problem with these two? Were they jealous? If so, of what? Her youth, her vigour, her artistic leanings, or her obvious intellect? Sarah couldn't work it out. As far as Sister Angela was concerned, it was all of the above. If anything, this was the catalyst for Sarah to question not so much her faith but certainly her vocation. For the next few months, self-doubt and introspection played on Sarah's 'inner sanctum' on a daily basis. As well as events inside the convent, there were other global issues that Sarah simply couldn't reconcile in her mind. A recent gun attack at a Primary school in America, one which Sarah found disturbing and frustrating. Disturbed at the number of innocent lives lost. What added to her frustration was that any time she questioned this with her seniors, they would not discuss it, leaving Sarah to question if they knew the background or bigger picture to any of this and, if so, did they even care?

The likes of this merely heightened Sarah's general feeling of claustrophobia. There was a big world out there, and she wanted to know more about it. One of the final nails, if there was one, was attending her cousin's wedding a few weeks earlier. While naturally pleased for her cousin Molly, she could not help but feel a hint of jealousy too, as she started a new life with her husband-to-be, with children to follow fairly soon, no doubt. However, the final straw was the incident or, more accurately, the altercation with Bendy a couple of weeks back. Truth be told, this not only shook Sarah but scared her, and from this point on, her exit was the inevitable outcome. So, what caused the outburst from Sister Benedict? It happened like this.

It was early on a Friday morning, and Sarah had just entered the office she used to do her accounts when Bendy burst in the door. She was out of breath from running down the corridor. Surprised at the sight of this was almost enough …but her ensuing behaviour, well, Sarah had not seen the like of it before anywhere, let alone the convent! Bendy had totally 'lost it'.

She was screaming, 'Did you see the note, the handwritten note?' She repeated this two or three times, almost apoplectic by now. 'There was a name and number on some paper left on the desk last night.' Sarah was in deep shock and could only stammer back a reply of sorts. She told Bendy that there was nothing on the desk when she came in this morning. The desk was all clear. Next, it was almost like an interrogation, 'Did you lift it? What have you done with it?' The veins in her forehead were almost about to burst as she screeched again, 'Did you lift it?' Now, a bit calmer, Sarah replied, a bit more assertively, 'Sorry, Sister, but I didn't see it.' Then, almost as soon as she had entered, Bendy bolted back out the door in a flash.

Jesus - what was that all about? Sarah was still shaking a few minutes after Bendy left. She went to the nearby kitchen and made a cup of coffee to try and settle her nerves. She felt like seeing Sister Colette or Angela but was scared to, so she left it. But the thing was …Sarah had not only seen the bit of paper but innocently and not realising its importance, put it in her pocket to bin it later. This, however, was something she felt better not to divulge. There was indeed a name and number on it, but all Sarah could remember was that it looked Spanish or Portuguese, maybe. She made another coffee, took it back to her desk and got stuck into her accounts.

It took about twenty to twenty-five minutes before Sarah's heart resumed its regular beat. At that moment, she knew her life in the convent was over. Notwithstanding the incident itself, which had genuinely scared her, this Irish girl needed to spread her wings; as someone once said, '*some birds are not meant to be caged*'. She was increasingly intrigued about who this person was on the bit of paper and what they had to do with the convent. That, though, would be for another day.

Back at the bar, as thoughts circulated, it took almost thirty minutes to finish her first drink. By now, the bar had filled up quite considerably. She went to get another drink, moving on to a bottle of cider. A young track-suited lad spoke to her at the bar. Sarah didn't engage in conversation but smiled politely. As she sat down, she saw the lad follow her gaze. It took a few seconds for her to realise this, but she had just been 'chatted up'. Again, this brought a brief smile to her face.

Her next thought would be, 'What job would she get'? Who would want an unemployed ex-nun? Not fully appreciative of it during her stint 'inside' but her chores had actually ably equipped her for something, 'office' work. In the short term, at least, this was to be her next 'calling'. In twelve months' time, she was fully determined to have started a career or university, with university definitely her preferred choice. Twelve months seemed a lifetime away for her. Would she get there? What would Sister Benedict think of this? The same Sister Benedict who once belittled her A-Level grades, saying, 'They're giving out A-Levels like confetti now'. Sarah wouldn't forget this in a hurry.

Sarah had one more drink before she called it a night. She was going to go to the phone box to let Rosie know she had finally done the deed but decided to wait until the following day as originally arranged. Rosie was not only her cousin but also her best friend and confidante. Rosie was a year older than Sarah and studying Business and Marketing at university in Belfast. She was, in some ways, the opposite of Sarah; maybe that's what made them click. Rosie was gregarious, always in a high spirit, and loved her nights out; she was a real socialite. A freckled, good-looking girl with striking auburn hair akin to Sarah's mum, she had plenty of friends and no few admirers from the boys. However, unlike many of her peers, she didn't get above her station; humility was her overriding feature. Rosie was responsible for Sarah's fleeting involvement with boys thus far. Rosie introduced her to or was at least the conduit for the few 'kiss and tell stories' Sarah had before her 'calling' called. One of these was Colin McCurdy, a local lad with whom Sarah went out with for six weeks in her lower sixth year. Before spiritual matters intervened, this would prove to be Sarah's only real 'steady' boyfriend.

It was obvious that Rosie would be the one she would tell in these circumstances. In the weeks prior, Sarah and Rosie had exchanged various phone calls and letters before Sarah decided to head for Civvy Street. Sarah and her sister did get on well and kept in touch, but they weren't total bosom buddies. Rosie was perfect for the role. Sarah couldn't tell her parents or Mairead just yet. She knew Mairead wouldn't be a problem and would probably welcome the news, as would her dad, but mum would be different. She simply couldn't think of a way to tell her, scared in case her mum would feel let down or betrayed.

Half-way through her bottle of cider Sarah began to feel tired, had another cigarette and set off for the hotel.

Subconsciously possibly, she sneaked a quick look back in the direction of the bar to see if her admirer from before was still around, but no, he was long gone.

When she climbed into bed at 11 o'clock, she was drunk, not on alcohol, but in mind and spirit. What a day. She was sound asleep in milliseconds.

Chapter 3

Northern Lights

It was 6.15 a.m. when Sarah stirred. This was the first time in years that she hadn't set an alarm clock. Her normal rising time was 6.00 a.m. for prayers at 6.30 in the convent chapel. When she checked her watch, she couldn't believe it. The expanse and comfort of the double bed had more than served its purpose. After the excitement and euphoria of the previous night, she felt a bit strange. For the first time in years, she had, in essence, nothing to do, no real focus, and strangely, no one to please.

She went for a glass of water. She only had two drinks last night, but not being used to this, she did feel some effects from her 'night on the tiles'. She thought again of her two pals, Colette and Angela. Had they heard the news yet? Had the letter been opened? Sarah was sure by now it had been, and so she wanted to ring in to speak to either of them but knew she couldn't—well, not just yet anyway.

She would soon have to call Rosie and implement stage two of 'operation stowaway'. Even though she was in time for breakfast, she didn't feel like it or the company that might accompany it. She returned to bed for a few minutes before phoning Rosie and setting off for the train. If everything were in place from Rosie's end, she would get the 11.30 train to Manchester.

Rosie was to take care of phase two. Rosie was the youngest of five children. The two eldest siblings of the family had gone to university in England and settled there. The oldest in the family was Martin, who was happily married with one child and lived in Leeds. However, it was Rosie's sister, Frances, whom Sarah was planning to stay with. Rosie was going to tell Frances of the events and ask her if she would mind putting Sarah up for a couple of weeks until she decided what to do with herself. Frances was like Rosie, fairly easy-going, and Rosie was very confident after Frances got over the initial shock that there wouldn't be a problem. Frances lived with her fiancé Lee, a local guy who worked as an optician in town. They had a smart two-bedroom flat in Withington, South Manchester.

After her quick nap, Sarah went to the lobby to phone Rosie. Rosie should have been expecting the call. Sarah was nervously giddy as she dialled the number. The ever-reliable Rosie was there to answer. They conversed briefly, with Rosie prompting and probing Sarah about last night's events. Sarah was selfishly more concerned with Rosie contacting Frances and getting her new digs sorted. They parted with Rosie reassuring Sarah everything would be fine and to ring her back in half an hour for confirmation. Sarah gathered her belongings upstairs before checking out a few minutes later. She sat in the lobby downstairs, willing away the thirty minutes. After twenty-four of the thirty minutes, she could wait no longer and called Rosie.

- 'Hiya, we're all sorted', shouted Rosie excitedly. 'Frances will be delighted to put you up for a while. She's working today but said she'd meet you in the Black Lion pub right beside Piccadilly station at 5.30….. with one promise, for God's sake, don't have any more surprises for her or she'll need to be worked with - Give me a ring this evening when you've settled in'.

Sarah was relieved. Firstly, she was glad that Rosie's plan had worked and secondly gauging by the tone of the call, Frances genuinely didn't seem to mind her staying. As Frances was a bit older than Sarah and had spent the last few years in England she couldn't say although a cousin, she knew her that well. She was still a bit scared of Frances's reaction, would she be annoyed or disappointed at Sarah's 'antics'?

Sarah had plenty of time to walk to the train station, so to kill a few minutes, she grabbed a paper from reception and a much-welcome *Silk Cut* from her bag to help settle a few nerves.

As she waited at the train station, she felt the full effects of the impending winter. An unforgiving and inexorable chill was meandering its way through the remaining scattered huts and benches. Almost everyone was wearing the latest earphones or an earpiece of sorts, listening to what Sarah assumed was some kind of music. Sarah would have to wait for such innovative aspects of popular culture.

The train journey flew by. Sarah was now thinking about what she would do with herself. Certainly, in the first instance, she would get a temporary job as an admin, but in the long term, who knows, she still had no real answers, maybe teaching. She disembarked at Piccadilly station. 'This place is massive', she said to herself.

She took her time exiting the train, trying to get her bearings. She asked someone beside her while walking where the Black Lion pub was. The response was cold…nothing. Sarah was instantly taken aback; no need to be rude, she thought. All she had ever heard was that northerners were meant to be friendly, but not this one. She made it out of the station to see a clear blue sky, another Manchester stereotype. Thankfully this time proved wrong. She took shelter from the cold at a newspaper stand as she put on her coat. She tried again, this time more formally.

-'Excuse me, sir, do you know where the Black Lion pub is?'

- 'Are you Irish chuck?', was the swift and friendly retort,

- 'Yes, Co. Antrim, if you know it'. 'I don't chuck, but I sure know where the Black Lion is. How could I not? If I spent more time working here than in it, sure I'd be a millionaire by now…. head towards the gardens, luv, and it's there on your left, can't miss it'.

'Brilliant, thanks very much', replied Sarah.

Sarah's faith in all things northern had been restored. She had met her first but not last 'angel of the north'.

He was right. The pub was only two minutes away. Sarah sat down with her trusted bottle of cider and cigarette. She was sitting at the window of the pub, watching the throngs of people pass her by. She never felt so anonymous in her life. A far cry from Ballycastle, where, like most small Irish towns, even the dogs in the street knew your middle name and star sign. This felt good. No one here knew she was a 'nun on the run'. It would be a good hour before Frances would be there. With it being a Friday, the street outside was especially busy; you could find the lot here, from; 'the young and the old', 'the good and the bad', and 'the suits and the grunge', forming a fine eclectic ensemble before her very eyes. As she looked outside, she wondered why they were all in such a hurry. Spittles of rain were now descending upon the hitherto dry road, slowly turning the tarmac from a charcoal mosaic into a swathe of liquid in a matter of minutes as the heavens purred and roared aggressively. Majestic. Welcome to Manchester!

Even though Sarah loved going home to Ballycastle, especially in the summertime, when its picturesque and aesthetic beauty was unparalleled in the country, she was so glad that she was going to a completely new town right now. Here, she could make a fresh start.

As she idled away the time, she thought about calling Maria Fernandez. This was the name on Bendy's piece of paper, whoever she was. Her train of thought, though, was interrupted by the sight of Frances outside, waving vigorously at her with a big smile. Frances came in and gave Sarah the biggest hug she had received in years. She smiled and shook her head.

-'Great to see you, Jesus; I couldn't believe it when Rosie called. Are you all right?'

-'Frances, I've never felt better', Sarah replied. As soon as Sarah looked back up at Frances again, she could see the resemblance to Rosie, something she hadn't remarked before. She felt relieved at Frances's reaction, knew she wasn't going to judge her and seemed genuinely glad to see her. Sarah looked up at Frances again…and in a flash to match the torrents outside, broke down and, for a full sixty seconds, cried her heart out in the arms of Frances. When the tears dried up, Sarah looked up again and apologised immediately and profusely. 'Sorry, sorry, so sorry Frances, I'm making a show of you, here in your own town centre'. 'Look, this isn't exactly Ballycastle Sarah; I don't know anybody in here, and do you know even better, most won't even notice… the joys of living in a city'. Frances then beamed a smile and said, 'You've had a whirlwind few days and, as my father would say, 'better out than in'…don't you worry about it, you have more guts than me, Sarah, that's for sure, here, can I get you a drink?'. Sheepishly and still a bit embarrassed, Sarah said that another cider would be great.

As Frances went to the bar, Sarah was mightily relieved at Frances's reaction. Knowing she wouldn't be a burden felt good, felt very good. When Frances came back, they began talking so much that they missed their intended bus at 6.00 p.m. Catching up was good. Frances, after a couple of initial questions, didn't interrogate Sarah too much and mentioned that she had already told Lee about it. He, too, was looking forward to her staying for a while; again, this made Sarah feel good. Welcomed and appreciated were commodities in short supply of late for her. Frances, although a science graduate, has been working as a travel agent since she finished college and really enjoyed her work. She talked so enthusiastically about it; the only downside was having to work every other Saturday. Sarah was excited about getting a job soon that she would enjoy as much, even in the short term. About an hour later, they headed off for suburbia, in the form of leafy Withington. She couldn't believe how talkative Frances was as she hardly came up for air.

When they arrived at the flat, Lee met them at the door and gave another warm hug to the receptive Sarah.

-'Sarah, we've got a spare room, and you can stay as long as you like, don't worry about that...in fact, it would be nice to have some intellectual company about the place for a change', he said in jest in the direction of Frances. Frances, though, hadn't heard him. As the night and weekend went on, this would prove to be very typical of the conversation and banter between the two. Lee, as it turned out, was the quiet one of the two, with Frances, as she had been in the Black Lion, continually muttering away in a continual yet harmless fashion. Lee would chip in every now and again with a quip from his sharp armoury of acerbic wit. Frances, usually still in mid-flow talking, would remain oblivious to most of it. Innocent, entertaining.

After Lee had already prepared dinner, Frances and Sarah cleared out her new 'boudoir'. It was almost 10 o'clock, and Frances asked Sarah if she wanted a glass of wine. Sarah, genuinely tired and also not wanting to get in the way, declined the offer, saying she would rather get an early night, which she did.

The following day, Sarah got up early and went into Withington to buy some bits and pieces, with 'make-up' being the number one priority on her list. Frances had mentioned they were having another couple around for dinner that evening, and she was welcome to join them. Initially, Sarah said no, but Frances insisted, saying it was very informal and that she would enjoy it. Frances said that her friend Hannah was really lovely even though she talked a bit when she was drunk, and her boyfriend was funny and sarcastic. Sarah laughed, thinking she knew another couple not too far away, just like that.

At 8 o'clock that evening, all five sat down for dinner. Lee wisely had introduced Sarah simply as Frances's cousin, who had moved up from London for a change of scenery. Thankfully, no mention of 'the sisterhood'. The night flew by, and Sarah was really enjoying the adult and stimulating conversation that ensued. A lot of this was news to her; interest rates, house prices, to how good Australian wines were now, until the inevitable happened. The boys concentrated on football and the girls on shopping. Beer and wine were flowing, Sarah was glad that Hannah like herself, enjoyed the odd cigarette. It was nearly 2.30 a.m. before Hannah and her partner, John, left. Frances was feeling tired, so they left Sarah and Lee to finish their glass before going to bed. They contemplated opening another bottle, but Sarah said no, as she had enough and was way past her normal bedtime. She was also still getting used to alcohol in such volumes. Sarah thought, would she ever meet someone as nice as Lee and have such a great home life as Frances and him? Time will tell.

Sarah went to bed; she had really enjoyed the night. She felt a bit drunk as she finally got into the cold bed. Not surprisingly, she went out like a light. She awoke then suddenly at about 9.00 a.m. Not surprisingly, she needed to go to the toilet, but more pressingly, she had the mother of all hangovers as well. She had overdone the wine. After only two nights out of camp, she had yet to build up the tolerance levels required for the outside world. She drank a couple of glasses of water as her mouth was carpet-dry. As no one else was up, she went back to bed.

As it turned out, she wouldn't wake again till just before eleven. When she got up this time, she couldn't believe the time. She had never got up at this time in her life. She felt funny, not from her hangover, which was now well-cleared thanks to the glasses of water. It was more guilt for lying in, but what had she to get up for now? Not much. After getting dressed, she went up to the kitchen. Frances and Lee were still in their dressing gowns, having for them a typically lazy Sunday. Brunch would be less sophisticated than last night's lean cuisine. Tea and Toast would suffice as they weren't fit for much more. They would eat later when they were able for it.

- 'How are ya ar kid?' Lee shouted to Sarah in his soft but distinct Manchester accent.

- 'Grand, a wee bit groggy, but grand, thanks',

- 'Did you sleep alright?' Frances asked.

- 'Yeah, great, thanks, Frances', Sarah quickly replied.

- 'Look, help yourself to whatever, cereal, tea, toast', Frances went on to say.

- 'Thanks, some tea and toast will be fine'.

Moments later Sarah was also enjoying her light brunch.

-'Did you enjoy yourself last night, Sarah?' asked Frances.

-'I did, I really did; I thought it would have been awkward, but they're a really nice couple. John's a really funny fella'.

- 'he has his moments alright', Lee replied.

Then Sarah looked up at the clock, and suddenly she shouted out, 'Oh my God. Oh my God', Startled, Frances looked over,

- 'What's wrong, What's wrong'?

Sarah put her hands in her face and said, 'I've forgotten to go to Mass', Frances and Lee looked over, aghast, not knowing what to do or say.

- Sarah then took her hands from her face, put them over her mouth, and started to giggle,

-'I can't believe it, I can't believe it'...her giggle turned into a more pronounced and uncontrollable laugh.......in seconds, all three were in hysterics, in tears, but thankfully tears of laughter. The red wine had put pay to prayers. Sarah really was now in the secular world, another mere mortal not making Mass on a Sunday morning. A casualty of Jacob's Creek, all the way from the land down under.

Chapter 4

Curriculum Vitae

On Sunday night, Sarah and Frances were hatching a 'masterplan' to get Sarah back to work. Sarah reckoned she would be best visiting some of the recruitment agencies in town. She hadn't realised that this would be a fruitless task without a CV. So, she would spend Monday doing this on Frances' home PC. Sarah hadn't really thought that far ahead, never having had to do this before. They also spoke about how and when Sarah would bring her parents up to speed. After some discussion, it was decided that Sarah would phone her mum the next night to explain all. The more she thought about it she was relieved it would happen soon. As soon as she got this over with, she really could start getting on with her life. Thoughts of the convent weren't too far away, though, as again she wondered what the reaction was to her departure. Here, Frances had another innovative, if not sneaky, idea. Sarah would ring up using the guise of a nurse in one of the local hospitals that Sister Angela visited. This way, she would be able to speak to Angela 'incognito'.

Putting together the CV proved more challenging than Sarah thought. She was getting distracted by some of the 'quality' morning tv on view, which was still very much a novelty for her. Eventually, by about 3 p.m., she completed the task. Satisfied with her day's work, she rang Rosie. Rosie informed her during their conversation that she had booked a flight to Manchester in a couple of weeks and told her to get her glad rags ready. This heartened Sarah no end, and she duly informed Rosie that she had just completed her CV and was hoping to get sorted with work by the end of the week. In good form after speaking to Rosie, she phoned the convent. After spending two years in Greater London, she was confident she could pull off a kosher English accent. Nervously, she rang the number and got through. It was Sister Ignatius who answered before passing on to Sister Angela who was obviously in deep shock at hearing Sarah at the other end of the phone.

-'Are you ok? ….Are you ok?' Angela spoke as quietly as she could, given the circumstances.

-'Look Angela, I'm really good, the best, I just had to get out of there'.

-'Where are you?' asked Angela, obviously still concerned.

-'I'm staying with my cousin in Manchester for a couple of weeks until I get sorted. Look, I hope you and Colette aren't mad at me, but I thought long and hard, and I thought this would be the best way'.

-'Don't worry, it's fine, I understand. Colette was a bit annoyed, all right, but she'll get over it; I'll tell her you said hello'.

-'What was said anyway…. did Bendy say anything?'… Sarah then asked inquisitively.

-'It was a bit strange; they waited until Sunday lunchtime before they said anything. They gathered everyone into the kitchen. Mother Superior just said very matter of factly that you had left for personal reasons and that your jobs would be redistributed by the end of next week. That was it. Angela and I knew something was up, but we weren't expecting all of that. Sister Benedict just tutted and muttered throughout …I think she was saying,… 'Disgraceful behaviour'.

We knew you were unhappy of late but we weren't expecting such drastic action. Look I better go in case someone comes in'.

-'Angela, I'll call again in a few weeks, God Bless', Sarah said before finishing the call.

Sarah wasn't surprised by the perfunctory performance of 'the soup' or Bendy's reaction; in fact, she would have been disappointed if Sister Bendy hadn't reacted that way. It wasn't as if they were all like that in the convent. It was only two from twenty-three, the rest were absolutely fine. Indeed, the vast majority, she believed, had a strong vocation and were contributing in their own small way to improving the lives of others not only in the community they were based but beyond as well, through their dedicated prayer. What Sarah just couldn't get was if Ignatius and Bendy were so unhappy in their lives, how or why they remained a nun. Sarah detested them both, but it was Bendy that had brought her to the brink.

This brought her back to Maria Fernandez, so she decided to call the number and see who or what she was. By now, Sarah had worked out it was a Spanish number, but that was about it, her 'Miss Marple' skills not yet fully developed. Not surprisingly, there was no answer, but the message on the machine was definitely in Spanish, and it was a direct line to Maria Fernandez, so I guess it was a start. Out of curiosity, Sarah left a message saying she was from the convent, etc…and left it at that. She thought part of the message mentioned the word Santander; whether this was the Spanish city or the bank, she wasn't sure. A bit sneaky to mention the convent? Yes, maybe…but she didn't really expect a callback, so she soon forgot all about it.

After a final read over the CV, Sarah was sorted. She had printed off ten copies as instructed by Frances, as she said there were so many agencies to go to in town. To repay the favour of Saturday night, Sarah made dinner for Frances and Lee and began to psyche herself up for the phone call to her mum.

By now, it was 9 o'clock and time for the call; Sarah started to have palpations even more than she had when she left the convent. She had even rehearsed her first three lines to make sure not to panic anyone too much. At 9 o'clock on the button, she took a deep, deep breath and called home. The call lasted all of five minutes. Sarah couldn't believe how well it went. Thankfully, it was her mum who answered and when she told her she wasn't surprised at all. Her mum went on to say that she knew she wasn't happy of late and had even told her dad a few weeks ago that this might happen. Her mum said, 'Don't worry…take your time to get yourself sorted, keep in touch and try and come home before Christmas'. It was as good as a confession to

Sarah as afterwards, she felt totally absolved. Whether it was women's intuition or not she was so relieved her mum hadn't a problem with her decision. Sarah didn't go as far as relaying exactly how she left the convent, covering the basics would suffice for now. That was it; she was now ready to take on the world, well, all the recruitment agencies in Manchester anyway and what they had to throw at her.

Chapter 5

Office Angels

Tuesday morning, Sarah began going through the tedium of visiting various agencies to hand in her CV and for them to ask the same series of questions in return. As she saw it, the main drawback would be how potential employers might react to her history in the convent. She would have to wait and see. Most, if not all, agreed with Sarah's assertion that her immediate future lay in some form of 'admin work'. They all said that she had built up some good experience and believed they would have an interview for her in a week or two. It all seemed promising. She knew the money wouldn't be great, but as she was staying with Frances 'gratis', she could soon save up for a rent deposit and move on.

On Wednesday afternoon, Sarah got her first call for an interview. It was for a large IT multinational based in town. They wanted to interview her on Friday morning. Sarah was delighted and excited, and with the help of her new friend 'Google', she did some research. It was only a temporary position, but she knew they might have other, more permanent opportunities if she got her foot in the door. On Thursday night, Frances and her were like two schoolgirls doing their homework as they prepared for the interview. Frances explained that most companies now tend to interview relatively formally and expect at least two people, one from the Personnel Department who would be taking notes. 'Don't be put off by that it's just standard now', she told Sarah.

As it turned out, the interview was a total disaster. Frances was exactly right in her presumption about the panel structure and formality, but when it came to it, Sarah just froze and couldn't answer anything. Initially disappointed, she knew at least how the game worked and knew it would prove beneficial for her next attempt. Not long after the interview, she got another call for another interview on Monday afternoon. This one was for a small construction firm again in town. Sarah was much more relaxed for this one as was the interview itself. This time, it was with the Managing Director, who interviewed alone, and she felt it went well. A niece of his was one of three who worked in their central office but had been out sick for a few weeks, so they wanted someone to help with their accounts. It was only for two weeks until the niece would return, but the limited tenure didn't put Sarah off; she just wanted to get stuck in.

A couple of hours later, back in the flat, Sarah got word she had got the job, and they wanted her to start on Wednesday. This wasn't a problem as she was keen to start earning as soon as possible. Their office was on Oldham Road, near the city centre. On Wednesday morning, Sarah arrived early and well-dressed on her first day, hoping to make a good impression. She was told to be there for 8.30 p.m. As she was early, she went for a coffee to pass away a few minutes. 8.25, she went over to the office. At 8.50, Sheila, the office manager, as she called herself, eventually emerged in a flustered state with a key in her hand.

-'Sorry, luv, that bloody traffic just gets worse and worse. You must be Sarah. Is Karen not here yet…where the bloody hell is she …she's never early, that girl…young ones, eh?'

Sarah, ever punctual, thought better not to mention to Sheila about her own tardiness, as it was her first day.

'First up, luv. We'll get a brew. Then I'll show you the ropes. Karen normally makes the tea, but I'll make one for ya as it's your first day'.

A few minutes later, Karen walked in, sat down, and turned on her computer without saying anything.

Sheila didn't seem to pay any notice but obviously had heard Karen enter. Sarah decided to break the ice by going over and introducing herself, as it was clear Sheila wasn't going to. Karen looked up as Sarah shook her hand, barely making eye contact before quickly glancing back at her computer. The atmosphere seemed a bit strange to say the least.

As per Sheila's instructions, Sarah's job was to work on customer invoices. Sheila opened the drawers beside her desk, where scores of invoices sprawled everywhere in no apparent order. Sarah first had to put them in some sort of order before she could make any sense of it. She did this, and it took nearly an hour to do. In this hour, there wasn't a word spoken between the three. Karen looked every bit her eighteen years and was probably the quietest, most introverted person Sarah had ever met. Sarah felt like she had left one convent to be snapped up by Manchester's only 'silent order'. Strange. Even the 'office' aesthetics and general look were not very appealing. It was more of a room that was evidently once lived in with the décor and furniture matching the atmosphere in the team.

The first word uttered in over an hour (apart from a telephone conversation by Sheila) was when Sheila broke the eerie silence.

-'Have you the Simpson file sorted yet, Karen?' Well, this certainly broke the silence, as Sheila was every bit as noisy when she spoke as Karen was quiet.

When the reply was 'no, not yet'…Sheila said it needed to be done by 2 o'clock and to ensure it was….'even if you need to work through lunch'. Sarah began to wonder what she had let herself in for. She felt sorry for Karen, who seemed so subservient to the demands of her dictator boss, Sheila.

It wasn't the homely family-run business Sarah was expecting, but at least it was only for two weeks, so she thought she might as well stick it out. Over the next few days, she couldn't believe how rude Sheila was to her youngest staff member. It brought her back to the convent, with Sheila at times as nasty and nefarious as the gruesome twosome she had left behind. Sarah also couldn't believe how disorganised the place was and couldn't wait until the two weeks were up. When talking to Frances about it, Frances assured her this was typical of small family-run firms, and her next job would be much better. However, it did prey on Sarah's mind, just when she thought she had cracked this 'normalisation', there was yet another stumbling block.

Thankfully, by the end of the two weeks, Sarah had gotten a longer-term contract elsewhere at one of the local health authorities. She thought it couldn't be as bad as the last place, which was a real eye-opener. For a time, she felt she was working in 'Fawlty Towers'. Her new post was to be in the Communications Department. The 'Comm.'s Dept.,' as it was known, had a Communications Manager and a Communications Officer. They were developing a new website, and this, along with a couple of other substantial projects, meant they needed some extra help. Sarah's time at the convent replying to all letters on behalf of 'the soup' had stood her in good stead as she flew through the interview.

Sarah was very impressed by the Communications Manager, Nick, during the interview. He portrayed such a professional and business-like image yet remained very courteous throughout. Nick was flanked by Darren from Personnel, who took most of the notes. This gave Sarah a good vibe, and she gratefully accepted the post when offered. She would work in tandem with the Communications Officer, the one and only Margaret McKechnie, from Paisley, on the outskirts of Glasgow. She soon settled into her new job as not only was there more structure to it, but she got on well with all the staff, especially Margaret.

Margaret, or 'Mags' as she liked to be known, had studied Art & Design in Manchester and had qualified three years ago, but by the end of the course, she didn't really want to pursue it as a career and somehow stumbled into communications. Her reason for not going into Art & Design was as only someone from Glasgow and Mags would say, 'there were too many fucking arseholes in it for my liking'.

How could you argue with that, this Margaret was not for turning. This was one of the many aspects that Sarah enjoyed about Mags: her directness. She said things precisely as she saw them, and no matter who the recipient might be, no holds were barred. Maybe this is also why Mags got on so well with her boss, Nick, as they indeed were polar opposites in terms of personality. Mags was full of life and had all the bubbly characteristics of her cousin Rosie, as well as having a loud but very infectious laugh. She was pretty small and chunky with black, wavy hair. In summary, she was a small girl but a giant personality. Sarah was in awe of and admired her confidence, general irreverence to life and little ability in her job.

The office they worked in also housed the Finance and Personnel teams, which had about forty people in an open plan, yet they had sectioned out the office. It would be fair to say Mags was probably the loudest yet most liked of the lot. Although she had turned her back on the whole Art & Design world, you could still see traces of this in her clothes. She got an awful lot of 'stick' about this, but this didn't matter to Mags as she gave as good as she got. She insisted on 'Mags' from the moment she was introduced to Sarah. Mags did seem to suit her better than Margaret and more befitting of her bohemian past in academia. On her second day there, Sarah felt comfortable enough to tell Mags about her own background. Mags couldn't believe it and immediately started apologising for all her expletives from the last twenty-four hours. Sarah just laughed and told her not to worry. She was now looking forward, not back. Mags promised if that was the case, she would get her sorted with a good local 'Manc' as she had done herself. Sarah mentioned that she had a cousin coming over for a weekend soon, so Mags announced they would need a girlie night in town on Friday night as a trial run. 'Irish doll, we're going to rock Manchester on Friday night; buckle up, kiddo and enjoy the ride'. Sarah knew she had met a diamond in Mags and was so looking forward to the weekend.

Chapter 6

The 'Comms' Team

Sarah enjoyed the department's people as well as the work itself. She had her fair share of basic clerical duties but was also given the scope to get involved in some of the more important and interesting projects, like designing the new website.

The hospital was convenient and accessible from where Sarah was staying. It was ten minutes on the bus followed by a five-minute walk, things couldn't have worked out much better. Mags rented a house with two other girls in Whalley Range, near Sarah's base in Withington. Mags was very friendly with Alex, one of the girls in the house, a psychiatric nurse from Wallsend in the Northeast, who also worked at the hospital.

On Friday night, Mags and Alex went out for a curry before going into town. Sarah, a virgin of such spicy food, agreed to skip the curry but would join them later. This was Sarah's first night out in town, and she was looking forward to seeing Manchester's nightlife at close quarters. She could even try out her new make-up and thought it would be helpful to get a good nosey around before Rosie's visit. The three were to rendezvous at 10 o'clock. Sarah, not wanting to be there first as she was on her own, made it there for ten past the hour and spotted the deadly duo as soon as she entered the bar. They had arranged to meet in one of the student bars at the bottom of Oxford Road to hit a club later on. After a few drinks, the spirits were good. Mags was on a mission, and she kept telling Sarah all week. She wanted to get her sorted with a bloke. As they sat, they critically evaluated all the males passing them by. For Sarah, it brought her back to her teenage days before she committed herself to the convent. It was fun, it was exciting, she was lapping it up. They had to drink up and head to the club in no time, with all three getting a bit 'tipsy'.

At first, in the club, Sarah was taken aback not only by the noise but by the sheer carefree spirit in such abundance. She was viewing all the sights on show, most wearing much less conservative garb than she was used to recently or Ballycastle for that matter. There were two different levels, both huge to Sarah's gaze, with the flashing lights a tad more extravagant than she was used to in the 'Castle Bar' back home. The noise and persistent beat of the dance music was a bit too much for Sarah, and she contemplated leaving the other two to it. Mags, though, was having none of it and was destined to get her set up with someone despite the merciless pleas from Sarah. Although glad Mags was looking out for her new friend, in reality, Sarah felt she had enough to get accustomed to a brand-new life without the added complication of a boyfriend at this early stage. Finally, some

R&B music came on, which pleased Sarah no end. Alex then decided it was time for a few shots. Sarah, remembering her hangover a couple of Sundays ago, wisely declined as Mags and Alex went for it, big style. After a bit of dancing and some cigarettes, Alex went to the toilet. Mags, by then, began to slur her words slightly, and said to Sarah,

-'I've something to tell you, and I hope you're not offended. Alex and I sometimes smoke the odd joint, nothing too major, just a bit of weed; hope you don't mind?'

Sarah replied swiftly,

- 'What….of course, I don't mind….sure there's no real harm in all of that'.

-'Brilliant' said Mags, 'I knew you wouldn't mind' … before going on to say in her broad Glasgow vernacular,

-'Do you know this Irish doll? You're a top girl, Sarah Delaney, a top girl', before hugging Sarah. Sarah could do nothing but laugh to herself, glad that she and Mags had become such stellar friends and not minding one bit getting her surname wrong. Delaney, Delargy, what's in a name! Sarah took this as her prompt to go; she bade farewell to the two and headed for home, smiling to herself most of the way. She had enjoyed her night out, hoping she would have plenty more of these with the 'Jock and the Geordie'.

The remainder of the weekend proved to be fairly quiet for Sarah. She went to Mass with Frances on Sunday morning, and the remainder of Sunday was a lazy day. Lee had gone out with a few mates to watch the 'Sky Super Sunday' game, so Frances and Sarah had time to chill out and read the Sunday papers at their leisure. They were both now eagerly awaiting Rosie's arrival.

At work, Sarah got all the gossip from Mags on Monday morning teatime. Not long after Sarah left, a couple of local lads came over to talk to them. This wasn't that uncommon when Alex was around. She was a tall, striking, good-looking natural blonde who often caught the eye of the male protagonists. She was from as far North as Newcastle, but she might as well have been from Sweden. In truth, the girls weren't really interested. Still, Mags, as ever, was enjoying the banter before a sudden nauseous moment came over her, and a quick visit to the toilet was required, where she relieved herself of some of the excess curry from a couple of hours before. When she returned, maybe wisely, the two lads had 'scarpered' just as quickly as her curry had scurried.

Chapter 7

Enjoying Work

Sarah was really enjoying her life in the Communications team. There were a few reasons for this. Firstly, the work itself was much more interesting and rewarding than the tedium of paying countless invoices in the 'madhouse' on Oldham Road. Secondly, she was beginning to get to know the others in the office and, more importantly, the dynamic and 'office politique' that inevitably went with any such job. Not surprisingly, Mags was at the hub of much of the banter rife there.

Sarah, although not getting directly involved, appreciated the craic and general 'bonhomie'. Not that it was always plain sailing, as in any office, there were a few highly strung individuals like Carly in Accounts, of whom Mags recently said, 'even her own mother couldn't like her'. Carly was from the Wirral outside Liverpool and unapologetically retained a strong 'scouse' accent. Mags had enlightened Sarah to the 'ones to watch', 'the ones to say very little to' (other than the odd porky) and 'those whom she just ignores'. Sarah was glad of the insider knowledge and basically kept her head down, trying to impress.

For the first few days, Sarah found it strange that there could be so much banter in the office, yet simultaneously, everyone seemed to get on with their work. Banter at work was a more restricted commodity in the serene confines of her convent days. There was another major reason she enjoyed her work: Nick. Nick Roberts was the boss and managed both Mags and Sarah.

Nick was in his early thirties, originally from Leicester in the midlands and a mad keen rugby fan. According to Nick himself, he was a 'dashing winger' in his day. For Sarah, he was dashing all right. He was a good six foot with blond floppy 'pop-star' hair. What attracted him to Sarah was not only his good looks, but he oozed confidence and all the charm and swagger to go along with this. Strictly in a work capacity, he also impressed Sarah no matter what issue or question Mags or she would have for him. He seemed to have an immediate and obvious answer. Nick, at the end of the previous week, had a quick chat with Sarah, and he gave her some excellent feedback about the quality and enthusiasm she brought to her work. When Sarah came back from his office on Friday, Mags jokingly said to Sarah, 'You were a long time with Nick, young Delargy, I hope you weren't getting any preferential treatment'. Immediately, Sarah blushed; thankfully, Mags had said this without looking up from her computer. Otherwise, it would have been an awkward and acutely embarrassing moment for Sarah. Sarah felt like mentioning her 'crush' to Mags but then thought better of it as she wasn't sure that outside of work, Mags liked Nick. She would often mimic how he flicked back his hair in an exaggerated, provocative style. Occasionally, in the confines of the office, she would refer to him as the 'beautiful one'. With Nick not only her boss and having a girlfriend, Sarah knew it would never be a runner. Wisely, Sarah focused on her new job and was encouraged by his positive feedback, so her confidence in the role grew. This was in no small way aided and abetted by the selfless Mags, who proved to be an excellent tutor and mentor all in one.

Although enjoying her time at the Health Authority, this didn't stop her from reflecting on life in the convent. Sarah may have been glad to have moved on, but with the chaos and turmoil now settled, her mind wandered more and more to Sisters Colette and Angela and the good times she had there. There was even a sense of guilt nagging at her when she thought of Angela and Colette relentlessly working away at their chores, helping the local community however they could.

Her time with Frances and Lee was also enjoyable. They seemed an ideal couple in almost every way. Although being hard-working, professional people, they were very 'easygoing' with neither taking themselves too seriously. They had a great apartment, only fully appreciated by Sarah after seeing the house that Mags and Alex rented. Frances' apartment was impeccably decorated with a fine mix of art nouveau and retro in every nook and cranny. The wonderful collage of colour and fresh carpets set the tone for the remainder of the apartment. However, each evening when Sarah returned from work, she found the smell most welcoming. Frances had 'pot-pouri' and Jasmin strategically placed in all of the rooms permeating an enticing and welcoming aroma every time you entered, a far cry from her recent past. Had she made the right decision? Yes.

Sarah had said to Frances and Lee a few times about moving out, but they would instantly and genuinely dismiss this. Lee especially went out of his way to reassure her there was no issue with her remaining there. Sarah did try to be as unobtrusive as possible, but no matter what Frances and Lee would be doing, Sarah would get an invite. Graciously, she would often refuse. Lee was such a cool and relaxed guy; she knew why Frances, a fine-looking girl in her own right, had fallen for him. Sarah then made a deal with them that she would stay until Christmas, giving her enough time to put away some money for a deposit to get her organised with digs of her own. Sarah, after all her turmoil, was in a good place, content. She had started going to the local chapel some evenings to pass the time. She may have lost her love for the convent but believed she wouldn't lose her faith.

With the weekend approaching, Sarah decided to sit in. Despite being recently paid, she felt she should start saving, and with Rosie due over next week, there would be enough 'partying' then. This was helped by the fact that Mags was planning to spend most of the weekend with Graeme, her boyfriend, and Alex was due to work nights. Sarah was intrigued by Graeme and could only imagine who wore the trousers in that relationship! However, when she had asked Alex about Graeme, she didn't seem overly enamoured. Well, to be truthful, it was more his group of friends she didn't like, as she felt they were a bit too 'arty' and 'lefty'. Sarah wasn't exactly sure what Alex meant by this but was still keen to meet him at some point in the future. When Sarah later pressed Alex on this, she gave her a curt response - 'Look, Sarah, Graeme's alright, but the rest of them, whatever you do, better to avoid them if possible'. Sarah, a bit surprised by Alex's reaction, thought it best to leave the conversation at that.

Sarah's plans for a quiet night would soon go astray. On Saturday night, Alex fed up with nights, called a 'sickie' and, not long after, called Sarah. It took all three seconds for Sarah to agree to a couple of drinks in town. They arranged to meet at 10 in the same bar as last week.

It was deja vu alright, as when Sarah entered at ten past the hour, Alex was in the same place. They hugged briefly before Alex began.

-'I'm sorry about phoning in, but it's been well over a year since I had a sick day. You know.' At that point, Sarah interrupted her.

'Look Alex, I really don't care, I'm not God, you know'. This made Alex laugh.

'Okay, Delargy, what you want to drink then if you're not God...Sex on the beach?'

'A wee cider would be great, you cheeky monkey', was Sarah's response, her turn to laugh.

In time, the conversation meandered its way to men. Alex was saying to Sarah that she had just finished a long-term relationship, so for now, she wasn't really looking for someone; she was just happy to go out and enjoy herself.

She then asked Sarah if she had her eye on anyone at work. Candidly, Sarah replied.

'Do you know there is, and I know it's not going to happen, but I think Nick, our boss, is really lovely'.

A bit surprised, Alex responded, 'The beautiful one'. Alex went on, 'I've only seen photos. He is hot all right, but I never really thought you would have gone for him. Mags reckons he's full of it, cocky like'. Sarah laughed and said,

'You did ask...there's also one or two doctors, but I haven't got to know them'.

'Not yet, Delargy, not yet', Alex said as she clinked Sarah's glass, followed by a suggestive wink.

As the night progressed Sarah couldn't help but notice almost every other male taking a second glance at Alex as they passed. She felt a bit in awe of Alex. Not only did she look good she was effortlessly dressed to kill. Radiance personified.

At that point, Sarah thought she would do a bit of spring cleaning on her own wardrobe as she was now paid and also in anticipation of next weekend. After a second drink, Alex suggested they go to another bar in Piccadilly. Sarah was fine with this but said she wasn't dying about going to a club.

Inside Alex went to the bar for drinks as Sarah took the opportunity to play with her new mobile phone. Calling and texting were as much as Sarah could manage up until now, when she was interrupted by a young lad.

'Hiya—what's the story? Are you looking for my number kid?' Startled, Sarah looked up and spoke.

'No', No'.

'I don't bite, luv, don't worry' was the unimpressed response.

Sarah immediately apologised and smiled instinctively, then held out her hand and shook her new friend's hand.

-'Cheers, but I didn't know I was meeting the Queen'.

Sarah, aware she was a bit formal in her introduction, laughed then responded with, 'I'm not the Queen, but you look a bit like Prince Charles'.

'My ears aren't that big', was the reply as they both laughed, this began a conversation of some note between the two.

A couple of minutes later, Alex made her way back to Sarah before spying her, mid conversation. Pleased that she was engaging with a good-looking young lad, she decided to sit back and see what happened. Sarah had gotten fully engrossed in a conversation on her own, probably for the first time since her new life began. Belatedly, Alex then made her way back, purposely not interrupting their conversation. By now, bizarrely, the conversion had moved on to the merits of Tony Blair as Prime Minister. Soon after Alex returned, Rob, as the politics student turned out to be, left, as summoned by his mates. Alex quizzed Sarah about him for a few minutes and was sure that Sarah liked him. She did, 'pity he was as pissed as a fart though', she sighed.

'Sarah pet, between that smile of yours and your Irish brogue, you're going to break a few hearts in Manchester', Alex proclaimed. 'I dunno… I wish', replied Sarah hesitantly.

They had another drink and headed for home. Inwardly, Sarah felt good. She enjoyed her banter with Rob, and if it had not been for an excess beer or three on his part, she would have been tempted to take things a bit further.

Sunday was a slow, quiet day. A trip to the cinema was the height of her excitement. On Sunday evening she thought again about the elusive Maria Fernandez and as she hadn't heard any word back thought she would leave one final message. If she didn't get back after that, she would leave it.

Chapter 8

Office Anguish

On Monday morning, Mags, as ever, was keen to find out about Saturday night's events from Sarah. She briefly talked with Alex but wanted to learn more about 'Rob the student'. Sarah told her that there wasn't much to tell other than he seemed like a decent lad but was a bit drunk and probably wouldn't see him again. Mags seemed to be on a quest to get Sarah hooked up with someone and reaffirmed this by proclaiming how next weekend when Rosie came over, she would ensure she introduced them to some local talent.

At work, things were beginning to get really busy. The launch of the website was getting nearer, and Nick was beginning to place more duties on Sarah and Mags. This she didn't really mind and Sarah found herself staying behind some evenings to keep on top of things. Mags, although exceptionally diligent and competent in her role, left at 5.00 on the dot every day. Sarah didn't mind staying a bit later, even though it was unpaid for her as she wasn't a permanent employee. She was enjoying her work and, more importantly, felt she was really contributing to the team.

One evening, when working late, Nick came into the otherwise empty section of the office at ten past six to see Sarah working away. Surprised to see her, he remarked,

'Have you got your sleeping bag with you Sarah?' Sarah a bit startled looked up and nervously replied… 'oh aye'. Nick continued. 'Sarah, I appreciate all your efforts but there's no need to stay behind, you know we can't pay you overtime'.

'Nick, I don't mind; I'm trying to reconcile all the website expenditures to ensure we're within budget'. Nick replied, 'I don't need that until Wednesday afternoon, so don't worry and get yourself off home'.

Sarah agreed and started to tidy up as she went to shut down her computer. Nick then asked her if she was enjoying her time in the department. Sarah said that she loved it, especially as she and Mags got on so well professionally and personally. Nick shook his head and smiled, 'Yep, she some girl is our Mags, sometimes I think she's the boss…she certainly keeps me on my toes'. The conversation continued with Sarah explaining how this was so much better than her first job on the Oldham Road, to life with Frances and Lee, to some of her nights out with Alex and Mags. It only came to a halt when Sarah, seeing the time, now almost 7 o'clock, exclaimed she would need to get home as Frances would think she was lost. 'No worries, safe home, and I'll see you tomorrow', said Nick as he left Sarah to make her way to the bus.

Sarah couldn't believe how the time had elapsed so quickly. Similarly, she couldn't believe how easy she found talking to Nick. She had an extra bounce as she walked to the bus stop. She had really enjoyed her conversation seeing a very different side to Nick. Here, he wasn't the brash, uber-confident manager; instead, he came across as a friend genuinely interested in how she was. Her heightened feel-good factor continued the whole way home. The truth was that if she hadn't fancied Nick before, she certainly did now. The more altruistic side of Nick that she thought he probably didn't have ensured she was 'snared'. She wasn't the first in the office and not the last who would admire the talented Mr Roberts.

As Sarah entered the apartment, she was still on a high of sorts, adrenaline still engulfing her heart, mind, and soul. Frances was quick to ask if anything was wrong as she entered the living room.

'No. No, I was just working a bit late, then the boss came in, and we just sat chatting for a while'. Now intrigued, Frances pursued the matter a bit further, and she was interested to know a bit more about this boss of hers. Sarah told her all about Nick and what they had talked about. Frances then remarked, 'he seems a bit of all right; I hope you don't have a bit of a crush now, Sarah'.

Sheepishly and unconvincingly, she replied, 'Oh no, he's just a good boss to have'. Frances knew better but decided to leave it, not wanting to be seen to dictate or preach to Sarah. Sarah then closed the conversation by saying, 'Frances, to quote from the bible, he's 'forbidden fruit', he's my boss and has a girlfriend… but a girl can dream a little, can't she'. They left it at that as Sarah went to the kitchen to prepare her dinner. Frances, though, was inwardly worried that the very same fruit might someday be too tempting to resist.

On Tuesday morning, Sarah didn't want to mention anything to Mags about the previous evening, knowing she would only 'wind' Sarah up. What the conversation did do for Sarah was to hasten to close out one of the outstanding parts of her 'normalisation', meeting up with and 'snogging' someone she liked. It had been well over two years since she had been remotely intimate with anyone, i.e. a quick snog at the Castle Bar back in Ballycastle. This made Sarah feel nervous, nervous but also excited. She was hoping this weekend would be as good a time as any, especially with her mentor of old there, cousin Rosie. With the weekend in mind, Sarah booked Thursday afternoon off to go shopping and visit the hairdressers. In the weeks since she left the convent, the hairdressers were something Sarah just hadn't got around to doing. Even though she was busy at work, she felt the week drag a bit, so much so that she was looking forward to the weekend and meeting up with Rosie again.

All was going well until Thursday morning, when Sarah got an e-mail, she did not appreciate from Carly in the Finance team. As planned and on time, Sarah completed the weekly report on all purchase orders spent on the new website. So, before she finished on Wednesday and as instructed, she sent on to Carly, or so she thought. Distracted at the time by another one of Mag's comic sideshows, Sarah had sent the e-mail including some background information about the figures but had then forgotten to send on the actual spreadsheet itself. A simple and common enough mistake to make. It would have been fairly obvious that this was a simple mistake, or so Sarah thought. She couldn't believe it when she received Carly's reply the next morning. Rather than replying to Sarah directly asking for the missing spreadsheet, she had copied in 'half the world' in her reply. She had, among others, copied in the main accountant, Finance Manager, and Nick, her own boss.

Bad enough as this was, she had also commented about how, as she now hadn't received this on time, she would miss other deadlines later in the week. 'Bullshit', Sarah thought to herself, as she read the e-mail. Sarah was livid as she scrawled down through the mail in disbelief. Immediately, Mags sussed something was up and asked Sarah if she was alright. 'Look at this, look at this', Sarah exclaimed in an excited yet aggravated tone, 'I'm in big trouble here'. Mags read the mail and shook her head.

'That wee cow, that's so fucking typical of her, there's no need for all that'…. Mags was in mid-flow when Sarah, now in tears, upped and headed for the toilets. Thankfully, as they were right beside the door, no one seemed to notice as Mags went after her. Mags let Sarah open the floodgates. A minute or so later, when she had stopped, Mags, the ever-faithful ally, tried to reassure Sarah she had done nothing wrong, wasn't in trouble, and her simple mistake would be rectified in seconds by another e-mail. At this stage, Mags went into a rant and heaped a tirade of abuse at Carly. Her ears would be in meltdown if she had heard the half of it.

'That wee fuckin Barbie doll, she does this all the time; if you make the slightest mistake, she copies all the managers in the place, insecure that's her problem, the wee bitch. I swear some night we're all out; I'll take the heed clean aff her'. Now startled, Sarah had to try to calm Mags down. As so often happened with the two, when Mags eventually calmed down, the two were soon in stitches laughing about it. Order was restored. Mags told Sarah to send the report to all those concerned and apologise, and everything would be okay.

When they returned to the office, Sarah did just that, thought nothing more about it, and continued with her work. Mags was still muttering away about Carly, as they could just about see her at the opposite end of the office.

Now, back composed in herself, Sarah was more surprised than angry about Carly's actions; they were essentially the same grade, even though Sarah was a 'temp'. Why did she make such a 'song and dance' about this and bring it to the attention of both managers? Reassured by Nick's recent comments and Mag's words about Carly, Sarah decided not to let it get to her and put it down as a learning experience. Mags though hadn't quite finished,

'I don't know how Darren can put up with that', tutting in near-perfect rhythm with her typing. Darren was the recruitment officer and interviewed Sarah and Nick. Darren seemed like a nice enough guy, but it was Nick, for obvious reasons, who made the more significant impression during the interview. Seemingly, Darren and Carly had been going out now quite a few months. In many ways, similar to Sarah and Mags, Darren and Carly had contrasting personalities. Carly was, as Mags had proclaimed, 'Barby-esque'. She was slim, a pretty blonde with all the style and bling to match. Even Mags would have to admit she was pretty. It was her diva-like screeching accent that did it for Mags; in short, Carly was too much of a drama queen for Mags. 'Like all Barbies, she should be seen and not heard that one' was Mags' final quip on the matter before she headed off to a meeting with Nick.

Darren, on the other hand, was very quiet, yet seemed to be very popular with everyone in the wider department. He didn't make much of an initial impression with Sarah, but as he would occasionally join Mags and Sarah for afternoon tea, she began to see why he was popular. Mags liked him a lot, and the two of them enjoyed some great comic banter. Behind Darren's public unassuming persona, there was a great sense of humour and very quick wit. In fact, he was probably the only one who could get the better of Mags. Darren was of average height, average trim build, with short brown cropped hair. When you did get up close to him and get to know him, he was fairly attractive in his own right, with bright blue eyes. Sarah had tried to push Mags on whether she had a soft spot for Darren, but she would never bite, saying he only joined them for tea as his interviews often overran, and he missed his normal break time.

It was nearing lunchtime and Sarah was looking forward to her shopping spree when she received another e-mail about the Purchase Orders, this time from the Finance Manager. '*Shit*', Sarah said to herself as she slowly, reluctantly opened the mail, fearing another rebuttal. Only this time, there was no rebuke. Ian Collins, the Finance Manager whom

Sarah had spoken to only a couple of times before, sent an extremely complimentary e-mail to Sarah thanking her for the detail and clarity of her report, stressing how this would make it very easy for the finance team to manipulate and process the end of month figures. Again, Ian had copied all those in Carly's initial mail. Sarah couldn't believe it and showed it to Mags on her return.

'Aye, put that in your pipe and smoke it, Barbie', she said after reading through. She went on to say. 'Jesus, I better watch you, Delargy, you'll be taking my job next.… only joking, fair play to you, you deserved that, and so did our little blonde friend'.

Sarah headed off into town without a care in the world. Her hair appointment was at 4 o'clock, so she had a good two hours after to pick up some bits and pieces. Mags had encouraged her to get some glitz and colour, and she would be 'knocking 'em dead' at the weekend. Sarah knew she needed to brighten up her civvy uniform, alright, but she would walk before she ran in this regard. Nevertheless, she was pleased with her few purchases as she made her way to the hairdressers. She was going to the same girl Frances had used for the last couple of years and didn't really know what to get done. Her hair, now shoulder length, was as long as it ever was. In the end, she left it to the stylist, Mandy; if she was good enough for Frances, she was good enough for Sarah. An hour later, Sarah emerged excited and pleased with Mandy's handiwork. She hadn't done very much, but after a few 'low-lights' and slight trim, Sarah felt a million dollars as she headed for suburban Withington. It was not a major transformation, but for Sarah, it made her feel like a movie star. In effect, it reignited her femininity and increased her inner confidence all in one.

At work, the next day, Mags and many more were complimenting her new look. During their morning break Mags began plotting the weekends itinerary. Darren joined them briefly before rushing off to more interviews. He too positively remarked on Sarah's new look.

Chapter 9

Cider with Rosie

Frances had agreed to pick up Rosie from the airport on Friday afternoon, expecting to be home around 6 p.m., the same time as Sarah. That evening, Sarah left work at 5.30 and set off for home. It was a bit after six before Frances and Rosie arrived. Lee had decided to go out for a curry after work with some pals, leaving the Delargy clan to catch up. A wise move for the ever-astute Lee, as all three sat for over an hour chatting, cackling away like three teenage school kids. Sarah's appearance took aback Rosie. Even though it was only three months since they last saw each other, Rosie couldn't believe how grown-up and mature-looking Sarah had become, no doubt aided by the recent visit to the hairdresser. Admittedly, Sarah has put on a couple of pounds in the last few weeks and months, giving her a slightly fuller figure, not a bad thing, but the recent wardrobe refurbishment and makeover had really done the trick.

Over dinner, Sarah explained the plans for the weekend. Tonight, they would have a 'quiet' night meeting with

Mags and Alex on Oxford Road and sample a bar or two. Frances politely declined the trip, leaving the 'youngsters' to it. Tomorrow would be shopping and heading out for a meal before clubbing into the early hours. Rosie had a late afternoon flight on Sunday, so she wasn't too bothered and was looking forward to her nights out in a new town. After hearing some of the antics of Alex and, more so, Mags, she couldn't wait to meet up with the formidable force from Paisley.

The four duly met up, with Sarah doing the introductions. The ever-affable Rosie soon conversed with Mags and Alex as if she had known them all her life. Mags told Rosie her quest for the weekend was to get them sorted with some local lads. Mags offered Rosie a cigarette as she did the others, with Rosie instantly refusing as she had never been a smoker and was a bit surprised at Sarah puffing away.

'I didn't know you were smoking again', Rosie said inquisitively, 'ach just the odd one, only really when I'm having a drink' replied Sarah. Mags soon chipped in, 'That means every night Rosie, mad as a hatter this one, you know, ever since she got out of Prisoner Cell Block H'. They laughed and sampled another couple of drinks before heading to another pub on Portland Street.

This was a lot busier, with a small queue to negotiate before they could enter. Not long in there, Mags was quickly at her impudent best goofing about with some of the lads inside. Soon, they were engaging with a few different groups, making their way to the bar, where the girls had settled. They had planned to go to another bar, but as time was whizzing by, they decided to stay put in case they would have to queue or, worst case, not get in at all. A few minutes later, one of the earlier group of lads made a re-appearance. There were three of them, one in particular seeming to have his eye on Rosie, finding her accent as beguiling as her smile. Mags was giving the lads a bit of a slagging as they had claimed they were all trainee Barristers,

'I hope none of yous have to defend me; I want my brief to have at least started shaving', before adding, 'then again, girls, at least they might look better with their wigs on'. She was hinting that maybe they were exaggerating their age as well as their profession. When probed a bit by Rosie, they did seem to 'talk the talk' about their job, giving some plausible answers. At this point, Mags dragged Alex and her off to let the Delargy girls get to it. The conversation seamlessly flowed, and soon, the three lads asked Sarah and Rosie if they wanted to go to a club. Both firmly said they hadn't planned to, just as Mags and Alex returned. Mags, on hearing the last bit, told the boys, 'Aye, these girls have been raving about going to a club all night; why don't we all go'.

Sarah wasn't sure if Mags was serious, she wasn't too bothered so asked Rosie if she wanted to go. Rosie, like Sarah, with another night to come, felt happy enough to go home as it was by now almost 1.00, and they had a good night. The night wasn't all in vain, though, as one of the more persistent lads swapped numbers with Rosie so they could hook up the next night. Rosie wasn't too bothered but more out of politeness took the number. As he was doing this, his friend, whom Sarah had spoken to sporadically, came and asked Sarah for her number. A bit taken aback, Sarah replied, 'No, No, I can't, I don't have a mobile phone'. 'Fair enough', was the casual reply. As the boys left for the club, the same lad hugged Sarah and said maybe we'll meet up again sometime...'Yeah, maybe', Sarah replied, still in a daze. She had just been thrown a curve ball. It had been a long while since she had been asked for her number so she was taken by surprise and didn't know what to do or say. Maybe more than the looks of 'Gary' her new friend, it was the strong aroma emanating from his after-shave that helped see him more appealing. It was pleasantly surprising and, more importantly, enticing...maybe she would see him again. Whether it was 'the wig-man' Gary or not, she knew she soon had to make some progress on the dating scene, even though she was still a bit wary about it all.

They headed for home, but not before Mags started to give off to Sarah. 'What did you say that for Delargy, I don't have a mobile phone, Jesus it's the twenty-first century everybody has a mobile'. Sarah just laughed and said, 'I didn't know what to say; he caught me off guard'...look here, Delargy, with the new hairdo and sexy outfit, you'd better get used to it'. They all embraced, went their separate ways and headed for home; a good night had by all. With all now exhausted, they went straight to bed when they got home.

On Saturday morning, Sarah got up first and made a 'fry-up' for all four. They had a lazy morning and a lazier afternoon where the Delaney threesome shopped till they dropped at the Trafford Centre, sandwiched by the odd glass of red wine.

The four girls had arranged to have a meal in town at seven. Drinks were flowing, complementing the fine cuisine on hand. Mags was trying to get Rosie to phone Marcus, who had taken her number the night before. Rosie said he should be trying to make the effort and left it at that. They made their way around to a bar in Piccadilly when Rosie got a text. '*Marcus, here sorry can't make 2nite but Gary and others are heading 2 the continental club later if use want to meet up, Good luck and c u next time maybe*? Rosie showed it to Sarah, 'There you go, you're sorted, Gary will be there waiting for ya. Mags mad keen to see the text, said, 'I know where it is …it's only five minutes' walk away, let's finish up and get round there to see Delaney the younger in action'.

It wasn't hard to know Mags was getting tipsy or worse as she was back to calling Sarah, Delaney instead of Delargy. Sarah, of course, didn't mind and tried to play down the thought of meeting up with Gary, but remembering the very alluring aroma of whatever scent he wore, she was secretly glad Mags had made the call to go to the club.

To the 'Conty Club' they went, as it was affectionately known by the locals. Mags and Alex had been there several times before, but not lately. According to the 'bard of Paisley', it was a haven for students, nurses and young professionals. Inside was an old-fashioned, dark, and dingy place, but simultaneously, it had a very relaxed atmosphere. Just the kind of place the Delargy duo appreciated. It wasn't a massive club, and as soon as they made their way to the bar, they saw Gary and two other friends of his. Greetings were quickly exchanged, and Sarah, after a few glasses of vino, felt less inhibited and was giving it loads in the conversation stakes. Again, there were four girls and three blokes, but Mags already spoken for, which meant this wasn't really a problem. Gary was a keen and good listener, just as well. The night flew by. In no time, the lights came on to pronounce the end of the night. When Sarah looked around, there were no Mags or Alex. They had already scampered, leaving her and Rosie with Gary and one of his mates. As she finished her last drink, she looked over to see Rosie now getting 'familiar' with Gary's mate. She felt awkward as she looked up at Gary again. He soon took the tension out of the air and, in a blink of an eye, put his arms around Sarah and began kissing her. Again, like her first cigarette on leaving the convent, her first kiss was also clumsy at first before she slowly relaxed into the moment. Bliss! Little by little, Sarah was 'breaking the habit' of her formal convent life.

Numbers were soon exchanged before the Delargy girls headed homeward.

The next morning, Frances was keen to find out about their night out, with Rosie only too keen to spill the beans. All three then went to Mass before a light brunch and some more conversation. In no time, it was time for Rosie to catch her return flight. Sarah tried to get her to come over again before Christmas, but Rosie, still a student, couldn't afford to. She, too, had a great weekend and would love to come back, but this, like all good things… would have to wait.

Chapter 10

Website Launch

By now, it was only a few weeks to Christmas, and the launch of the new website was fast approaching—the deadline was Friday, 30th November. This was a major event not only for Sarah's team but the wider function, so much so that the Head of HR & Communications called in one day to the team to say hello and thank them for all their work. Things were on track, but there were still loads to do. Even Mags was staying on a bit later some evenings.

Having stayed in the previous weekend to save money, Sarah was 'dying' to go out this weekend; either night would do, but Alex was back on nights, and Mags was booked up with Graeme and his pals. She eventually ventured out on her own with a trip to the local cinema on Saturday night as Frances and Lee were away for the weekend. Solitude, of course, was nothing new to Sarah, so she didn't mind going on her own, and at least it passed the Saturday evening for her - Match of the Day on TV wasn't really for her. She had contemplated ringing Gary but thought better of it, thinking she might bump into him some other weekend.

On the Sunday after Mass, she strolled around St Mark's Parish Centre. She hadn't realised there was so much to it, with many conjoined buildings making it quite the complex. She saw adverts for various arts and crafts, as well as one for the Senior Citizens club. The senior citizens could wait for a while, but Sarah was keen to return to her favourite hobby as she saw they also ran Art classes. This would be great for a night in the week after Christmas, another reason for her to hang around the Red Rose City. There was a hive of activity in one of the far buildings, and someone somewhere was cooking; the smell of a good Sunday roast was in the air. She 'noseyed' over and saw a large hall full of people getting their Sunday sustenance. She recognised one or two serving the food from Mass, remarking what a great atmosphere there was inside. Coming from a small rural town in Ireland, she was used to community spirit but didn't expect it here in a thriving metropolis. Her mind meandered back to Sister Colette and Angela and all the good deeds they do despite everything. A trace of guilt engulfed Sarah momentarily as, although she was not really missing the full rigour of convent life, she did miss the community outreach and help this provided. Sarah was in a bit of a daydream and didn't even notice Father Des Kelly right beside her. Ordinarily, he was hard to miss, he was six foot two at least, tall and slim with blonde curly hair and suitably bespectacled. He was the curate and, not surprisingly, a bit younger than the Parish Priest, early forties, Sarah thought.

'Can I help you, dear?' he said in his soft, lilting Cork accent.

'No, no, sorry, I was just…just…taking a walk around'. 'Aagh you're Scottish, I'm Father Des Kelly, nice to meet you, I've seen you at Mass a few times'.

'I'm Sarah, Sarah Delargy, actually North Antrim, so not far away from Scotland…but definitely Antrim'.

They joked for a minute about accents and passed pleasantries before Father Des said he had to go - it was time to serve desert. Sarah knew the church had many failings but also knew there were a lot of decent people still involved devoted to their parishes; Father Des seemed like one of them. She enjoyed his sermons too, short, to the point and often with a twist of humour.

She rocked up to work on Monday morning fresh and ready for a busy week with a 'go-live' date on Friday. However, there was a slight issue - there was no Mags. There was no Mags on the Monday and no Mags on the Tuesday. Not only did Sarah miss the 'craic' with her bosom buddy not there, but she knew with the deadline approaching, this might not go down well with Nick. It was Tuesday lunchtime before Nick told her that Mags wasn't feeling too bad and should be in tomorrow. While that was good news, Sarah was surprised and a bit disappointed that Mags hadn't at least texted her to let her know she was ill and wouldn't be at work. After Nick's update, she contacted Mags straight away, but by late that evening, still no reply. A bit perplexed, she texted Alex to suss things out - she texted straight back to say all was okay and that Mags was fine and would be in tomorrow but ended by saying, 'Don't tell Mags I said this, *but she was partying with Graeme and his pals*'. Sarah laughed to herself innocently; after all, she was a Glasgow gal, and they sure knew how to party.

The next day, Mags came in and, for a change, made a quiet entrance. Sarah glanced over, and despite looking like 'death warmed up', she wheeled her chair over to Mags and, without saying a word, gave her a long hug. Sometimes, silence is indeed golden. Surprisingly, for whatever reason, Mags was not as engaging as usual, so Sarah knew to back off a bit and give her some space. Mags went to the toilet and returned a minute later, still somewhat subdued but now more composed. She immediately apologised for not coming in as she knew she had left Sarah in the lurch with Friday fast approaching. Sarah told her not to worry; she did have to stay later the last two evenings, but all was in order, and she was only too glad to do some more meaningful and 'higher level' work. Mags looked over at Sarah and said, 'I'll make it up to you, Sarah; you better believe it…right? What do we need to do first?'.

The two girls worked like beavers for the next two days - they and the rest of the team did their trial runs by Thursday lunchtime, and everything seemed in order. Mags then did a presentation for Nick and the head of HR & Communications later that afternoon, including some formal trials. Everything was going to plan. At the end of the session, Mags went out of her way to thank everyone for their help, including the IT team and especially Sarah, who in no time in the team had got fully up to speed and without her help earlier in the week, the team wouldn't have been ready. Everyone in the room gave Sarah a round of applause, she was surprised; she didn't know where to look - not that you could miss her; once again, her face went flush pink with embarrassment. Mags was true to her word and her promise from earlier in the week. In a work environment anyway, Sarah had never been praised in public, her affection and respect for Mags was now supersonic, into a new stratosphere. With only the two of them now left in the room, a tear rolled down Sarah's cheek as she told Mags, 'You're unbelievable Mags, the best friend I could ever have'.

Friday morning was the acid test, though, and while there were a few grumblings and teething problems, things went well. Mags, no doubt relieved all had worked out in the end, was now more like her old self. Everyone was in fine fettle as there was a team night out already pencilled in in anticipation of all going well. Mags, though, had told Sarah she wouldn't be going, feeling she had partied enough last weekend. Sarah pleaded with her, but she was a definite 'no-no' for tonight. Then, out of the blue, she got an email from Nick asking her to call into his office at lunchtime. Sarah's face dropped; she asked Mags if she knew what it was about but said she knew nothing. Sarah ventured on and feared the worst, i.e. with the website all sorted, they might end her contract early.

Thankfully for Sarah, her fears were mislaid; in fact, it was the opposite; Nick told her as they were behind now on other projects, they would be extending her contract for another three months. Nick went on to tell her that he would love to make her permanent, but this was something he couldn't promise with budgets so tight, but he would work on it. He went on to say how incompetent the last few 'temps' had been and how different she was to them in attitude and competence. Sarah was delighted and felt like reaching over the table and kissing him - if only. On returning to her desk, Mags packed up as she had booked the Friday afternoon off. With a 'perma-grin' on Sarah's face, she told Mags the news. 'Well, no bother to you Delargy and well deserved…you want to have seen some of the clampets we had in here before you…you're worth about ten of them'. Sarah bid her farewell to Mags who was going home for a long bath and quiet weekend, insisting Sarah text her tomorrow morning on how the night went.

Sarah was on cloud nine as she made it back home. She made a quick phone call home to check in on her mum and dad just as she reached Chez-Frances. Frances sensed her upbeat mood, and Sarah soon updated her on her contract extension. Frances was delighted saying…' 'Sarah, listen to me now, you can be anything you want in this world, and don't you forget that whatever you want to do'. Frances, as ever, was reassuring and thoughtful all in one and was another boost to Sarah's self-confidence, which slowly but surely emerged after her convent days. So much so that Sarah decided to push the boat out with a recently purchased top that revealed some cleavage and a skirt much shorter than the norm. She wasn't keen on too much make-up for now anyway, but as she entered the living room, Lee did some 'wolf-whistles' much to the jest of all three. Sarah was beginning to find her femininity and to be truthful with her dark features, brown eyes and newly discovered pins to match, she didn't need much make-up to make heads turn. Frances then teased her again about Nick, 'I hope that isn't for the lovely Nick, our girl'. Sarah quickly reposted, 'I told you, Frances, forbidden fruit…..unfortunately', as they both giggled. However, in truth, Sarah was glad Nick was going tonight. Well, he kinda had to go as Team Leader, and maybe, subconsciously even, it was the reason for the wardrobe upgrade.

They were meeting at 7.30 in Withington, which, for Sarah, was much easier than going into town. The initial plan, if it went that way, was to grab something to eat and then hit the 70-80's night upstairs in the Withington Ale House. The restaurant was almost within walking distance for Sarah, but Frances insisted that Lee drop her off and get a taxi back. There were a good few out, maybe twelve in total, as Sarah arrived just about on time. She had no Mags to cling to but soon saw the posse in fine fettle at the corner of the restaurant. There was a spare seat at one end next to Ian Collins, so she said hello and sat next to him. Ian was an older man, short and stout, from Scotland originally, but he seemed a nice enough bloke, so Sarah was happy enough. It was Ian who had sent her the reassuring email a while back when Carly tried to land her 'in it' so she felt comfortable next to him. She saw Darren and the lovely Carly and Nick at the other end of the table, next to Amanda Khan, who worked for Ian in Finance and waved over to them all. Ian was indeed good company and shared some of his stories of his rural upbringing in Scotland, which Sarah could easily relate to. He was such good company, or maybe this was due to the cider now flowing, that Sarah, in hushed tones, told him all about the convent and her great escape. Ian was flabbergasted and looked at Sarah in amazement. 'What can I say…Wow! Amazing Sarah, that's just amazing, what can I say, I'm impressed….and for what it's worth, I think you've made the right move'. Sarah swore Ian to secrecy, which she knew he would keep.

By now, not only was the cider flowing, but Nick had bought a few bottles of wine for the team. Sarah was beginning to acquire a taste for the fine Italian Chianti courtesy of Nick. It was soon time for the 70-80's night, although by now, there was only a handful of hardy souls left willing to bust a few moves over at the Withy Ale House. Two small tables housed the party with Ian, Darren, and Sarah on one side, and Nick, Amanda, and Simi Kamara, who worked for Ian in Finance, were opposite them. Carly went home right after the meal to make things better, pleasing Sarah no end. Sarah was having the time of her life. Ian was not a dancer, but Darren was, although quiet and understated in many ways. He was sociable, and the boy could dance. Sarah and he were dancing the night away as the songs of ABBA filled the air.

Ian had left for home by the time Sarah and Darren sat back down. Fuelled by the vino and no little cider, Sarah started to question, well, more like interrogate Darren. It was all in good humour, even when Sarah asked, 'So how long are you going out with the lovely Carly then'? Darren laughed and said, 'I kinda get the impression you're not really that fond of her, Sarah'? With a glint in her eye, Sarah replied, 'Well, Darren Carter, since you asked, put it like this: she somehow doesn't seem to be on my Christmas Card list'. Darren laughed again and said, 'Do you know what, Delargy, I think you've been hanging around with Mags for too long; her sarcasm is rubbing off'. They both laughed and polished off another drink. However, as delightful and good company as Darren was, as the night progressed, Sarah's eyes kept wandering over to Nick's. She was sure he was aware and maybe reciprocating in kind… but yes, forbidden fruit. A few moments later, when the DJ put on Night Fever, Amanda grabbed Darren out to dance. There was no better man to ask than the Health Authority's very own John Travolta, who was lording it on the dance floor. Sarah now saw and seized her chance; she went to the seat beside Nick, vacated by Amada Khan. Small talk ensued for a couple of minutes; Sarah thanked Nick again for extending her contract, extolling the virtues of his wider team and Mags in particular. Nick was engaging but not flirting with Sarah; in fact, he seemed somewhat distracted by Darren and Amanda still on the dance floor. Sarah would not be deterred and bestowed further platitudes on Nick, now asking him about his rugby exploits. By now, it was approaching 1 a.m. and Sarah was undoubtedly drunk as she probed Nick further about his training regime and even how short were his rugby shorts! Nick was a bit surprised by Sarah's comments but knew this was probably the vino talking, so while not encouraging her, he kept the banter going. Darren and Amanda had by now returned from the dance floor and the ever-alert Darren had noticed that Sarah was getting a bit close for comfort. By now, she had her hand on his shoulder.

Darren rushed over and grabbed Sarah, almost forcing her to the dancefloor. Sarah, taken aback, threw her arms back at Darren and shouted, 'What are you at?…leave me alone, leave me alone'. Maybe there was some jealousy on Darren's part with the attention Sarah was giving to Nick, or more likely, he didn't want her to make an 'eejit' out of herself. That said, there were only a few of them left partying from the original group. Either way, words were exchanged on the dance floor for a minute or two. Darren pleaded with her to relax and come to the bar and have a last drink. Sarah was having none of it - in no uncertain terms she told Darren to go away and leave her alone. Sarah, without looking at a sinner, went back to her seat, grabbed her bag and coat, and took off down the stairs. Darren was in a state of flux; he was trying to do the right thing for her, but it backfired. He decided to follow her and try and get her a taxi but Miss Delargy had taken off like Usain Bolt. Darren looked on from afar, then followed her for a bit - he knew she was at least walking the right way home, and with the road well-lit, she should be safe enough.

7:14 a.m. - the next morning, Sarah awoke. She looked around in her small single bed; groggy, definitely groggy, bleary-eyed, yes bleary-eyed and tried to get her bearings. What ensued was a common enough experience for seasoned drinkers but new to Sarah - 'the morning after guilt-trip'.

As she sat up in bed, she felt her head begin to pound; the questions then started in whirlwind fashion:
- Jesus, how did I get home?
- Did anyone come back with me?
- Did I wake anyone when I came in?
- Was I sick when I got home?
- Did I make a fool of myself back in the bar?
- Did I insult anyone?

With her head still pounding, her stomach felt duly obliged to reciprocate in kind, with the 'washing machine syndrome' soon emerging down below. Next came a bolt to the toilet, and for two to three minutes, half the culinary delights of the night before went down the toilet. On her knees now and in a sweat, it was another five minutes before she had the confidence to stand up. Hearing the commotion, Lee was now at the door. That was all she needed.

'Lee, I'm so sorry, so sorry, I'll clean it all up'. Lee just laughed and said she must have had a good night. Lee knew it was not the right time for banter then said -'here, get back to bed ar, kid; I'll bring you in a glass of water; you'll be grand in an hour or two'. Double embarrassment for poor Sarah. She now sat in bed wondering, pondering what had happened ......the last thing she fuzzily put together was her and Darren dancing, then a bit later...Amanda is coming over to Darren...and then shit...Yes, she had gone over to Nick. What had happened after that - nothing! She couldn't remember a thing. She vaguely remembers a discussion of sorts with Darren. She'd text Darren...but it was far too early. Still, she needed to know, so she decided to go ahead.

*'Darren, what happened last night, I feel terrible….
did we fall out? Did I do anything stupid…so sorry!'*

Sarah waited for ten minutes but no reply - her mind was in overdrive. She only hoped Darren was fast asleep and not avoiding her. She then nodded off herself and awoke a good hour later. She heard Frances and Lee pottering about in the kitchen, felt a bit better so took a drink of water and checked her phone. Darren had come back.

'Hi hope you have a nice hangover lol - feeling it a bit here 2 - you were fine…we did fall out at the end cos you wouldn't dance with me lol. All good, I'll give you a shout on Monday morning sure'.

It slowly came back to her, Darren and her having an argument on the dance floor…but what happened with Nick - this would have to wait until Monday morning. She was glad that judging by Darren's text, things couldn't have been too bad. As Frances and Lee would jokingly tell her later that morning - it's always best to go easy on the red wine. Another valuable life lesson was stored for Sarah as she meandered her way through the maelstrom of secular life.

Come Sunday morning, feeling a lot fresher, Sarah went to Mass. After the service, she thought she would walk over to the large hall again and see what was going on today. Once again, they were serving food, which, as Sarah would find out, was a weekly occurrence. Seemingly, they served a full three-course Sunday meal for £3.00 – which was 'for nothing' in reality, a goodwill gesture for those not so well off in the parish courtesy of a local benefactor. That said everyone was welcome, irrespective of religion or from within the parish boundaries or not. She peeked inside and saw Father Des flat-out washing dishes, laughing with the ladies serving the hot food. Once again, it reminded her of home and the close-knit community there, and she thought she might seek out Father Des and volunteer her services. That she did, not long after entering the hall, and when she did this...meaning maybe some time in the future, Father Des said, 'no time like the present, Sarah, that's Yvonne and Anne serving, fire you away with the dishes here, I need to check the desserts'.

Well, how could she say 'No'? not one to be shy of work, Sarah soon got stuck into the dishes and, in no time, was brushing the floor, emptying bins and doing whatever needed to be done. An hour later, the four of them were finishing up when Father Des went over to thank her for her efforts and, in his acerbic dulcet tones, proclaimed to Sarah, 'Well, the pay is lousy, the hours are anti-social, but the 'craic' is always good'. Yvonne shouted back it should be the stage Father Des should be on, not the altar. Sarah replied that she'd be happy to help out any Sunday, every Sunday, if needed if they wanted. Father Des walked over to Sarah and, as only he could do, gave her a 'high-five' and said, 'You're hired, Miss Delargy. See you next Sunday', and with that, he turned on his heels and walked back to the parochial house also in the grounds. All three laughed; Sarah chit-chatted for a few minutes with the two ladies before making her way home. She felt good and thought Angela and Colette would be proud of her too - that gave her an inner glow, made her feel even better and put an inch to her step as she exited the complex.

On Monday morning, Darren was true to his word and called over to Sarah to fill in the blanks of Friday night. What Sarah didn't know, as only a few in the office did, was Nick having a bit of a fling with Amanda Khan the last few months…but more importantly, as she had surmised, Darren's intervention, although not appreciated at the time, had averted an incident with Nick and probably kept her in a job. She owed Darren for sure. Soon after, there was an email in her inbox, a reminder about this year's Christmas party - in a nano-second, Sarah had deleted it, a wise move.

As much as she was loving Manchester, she was really looking forward to a quiet Christmas back home - she had had enough excitement and turmoil in the last two-three months, some quiet nights in with a box of Quality Street would do just fine.

Chapter 11

Homeward Bound

By now, Sarah couldn't wait to get home for Christmas. She spent the next couple of weekends far away from Italian red wine and any alcohol for that matter. She enjoyed the next couple of Sundays over at St Mark's with her new three amigos: Father Des, Anne and Yvonne. Anne and Yvonne were her new 'Colette and Angela', and she had a right laugh with them, it was not like work at all. Sarah was also back doing some painting in anticipation of the impending Art Class in the New Year. Even Mags seemed to have calmed down the partying a bit, and as Sarah wasn't going to the Christmas party, Mags also reneged.

Enjoying the period of abstinence and to help while away the hours she was back devouring the delights of Dickens. Charles Dickens was easily her favourite author. More importantly, she was also spending weeknights viewing houses or, more accurately, rooms that she might rent after Christmas. She liked the Withington area and viewed rooms, some suitable, some not. She was getting increasingly frustrated when, for the ones she liked, none of the landlords would get back to her. There was only a week left before she was going back home, and as much as she liked staying with Frances, she was keen to give them back their space. Things were looking desperate, so she had started to look at some of the nearby areas that were not just as nice as Withington but had no choice.

When Frances happened to ask her about the house-hunting, she told Sarah to stay on as long as she liked but Sarah was having none of it. After Christmas was the time to move out and chart her own life. If this meant somewhere less salubrious than Withington, then so be it; after all, she wasn't exactly earning a fortune.

As it transpired, and not for the last time, St Marks would come to her aid. She happened to mention her house-hunting to Anne the next Sunday while tidying up. Anne told her not to worry; she knew a local estate agent who would sort her out, so it was no problem. True to her word, by the middle of the week, through Anne's pal, she had a room sorted. The house was about a ten-minute walk from where Frances and Lee lived. It was perfect. She didn't realise she would have to pay a month's rent in advance and a deposit to boot, but she was just glad to get somewhere. Her bank balance then took another hit, as despite warnings from Frances, Sarah dithered a bit on booking the flight home, and it was by now triple the original price - another life lesson harshly learned. So, with a slightly lighter wallet, on Christmas Eve, Sarah finally made it back to the rolling hills of Ballycastle and the green, green grass of home.

She had just over a week back home and loved every minute of it. Most of her extended family and locals knew by now that Sarah had left the convent, thankfully, though, not the finer details. She caught up with Rosie and her good pal from school, Clare Campbell. Clare was a nurse in Derry City, and they vowed to keep in touch.

With her mind much clearer, she enjoyed the time with her mum, dad and sister. Her dad, not really one for 'pep talks', feeling the pastoral side of things was best served by mum Anna, simply told Sarah that he was glad she had left the convent, and the world was now her oyster.

An additional visitor was in the form of her dad's brother, Tony. Tony was back home from Boston for the first time in a while. Tony was a year or two older than Fran but similar in many ways. Looks-wise, he was like Fran, though not just as tall and a bit quieter, but was still very sociable and a bit of a charmer in his own right. Tony had moved out there in his mid-twenties after a marriage break-up and hadn't looked back. By now, he owned his own Bar and Seafood restaurant and, by all accounts, 'coining' it in. Sarah had never really had an adult conversation with Tony but found him not only likeable but interesting, recounting some great tales from times in the bar back in Boston. He said to Sarah about coming out to Boston, but Sarah dismissed it. He said she would love it, and he remarked that unlike here, in the US, you can have a really good career in hospitality- if the locals like you - you could live on tips alone. Sarah could see why and how he was doing so well out there but thought this wasn't for her. Tony closed by saying how great it was to see her moving on with her life, and even if only for a holiday, she was welcome any time, and he would gladly look after the fare. It was a lovely gesture from Tony, who, despite living in Boston for so long, hadn't lost the accent, but maybe that's why he was doing so well. With his 'Yankee tan' he looked the picture of health, a warm look to match a warm soul.

As much as Sarah enjoyed her time at home, by the end of it she was looking forward to getting back to her new hometown. She had lots to look forward to; the prospect of getting a permanent job, her art classes, helping out Father Des at St. Marks, as well as the nights out with mad Mags and Alex.

Chapter 12

January Blues

Sarah hadn't made any New Year resolutions per se, something in convent life with so little vices you wouldn't really need. While home at Christmas, even when out a couple of nights at their local pub, the thought of a cigarette hadn't crossed her mind - so this would be an easy resolution for her. So, no more cigarettes; this time, she had no problem sticking to it.

She flew back on New Year's Eve, but Mags was still back in Glasgow, so there wouldn't be a big night out. Instead, she spent it packing her bags and belongings, limited as they were, ready for her 'flit' the following day. She was pretty much 'skint' anyway, so, as well as New Year's Eve, nights out in January would also be few and far between.

Frances had dropped Sarah off at her new digs. Sarah would be sharing with two other young professionals. Not surprisingly, with the hospital close, one of them, Adam, was a male nurse who worked there. The other was a friend of Adam's, Chloe, who worked in IT in the city centre. They were friends from college and had been staying there for well over a year. They were not a couple; despite Sarah's limited worldly antennae, she had already sussed Adam was gay - nothing wrong with that, she thought. They seemed nice enough, which was just as Anne had promised.

The next couple of weekends, Sarah immersed herself in her work and, at weekends, was still helping out at the church and doing some painting when she got time. Come the end of the month, not surprisingly, Mags was keen for a good night out. She had told Sarah that she had a really quiet Christmas, and as a surprise to Sarah, this was mainly due to the fact that Mags' mum and dad were pioneers - so Mags too was almost as temperate as her parents for the duration. By now, she needed a good night out and was hitting 'town' on Saturday night. As much as Sarah knew it would be a good night, she said no to Mags as she was still counting the pennies. Sarah's mum and dad over Christmas had both offered Sarah money to take back, but the resilient and slightly obstinate youngest Delargy refused. No doubt this trait comes directly from the gene pool of her dad.

On the Friday afternoon just before she left work, Sarah wished Mags all the best for her night out on Saturday before giving her a quick hug, a more poignant moment than she realised. As she headed for home, much as she would have loved a takeaway, she refused the temptation as watching her weekly budget. Over at her digs with Adam working shifts, Sarah had more interactions with Chloe, who, although quiet and introverted, was even good company anytime they shared the living room. Sarah's next modest but substantial purchase would have to be her own TV so she could have a bit more privacy and the ability to watch what she liked.

On Saturday afternoon, Sarah was strolling through Withington High Street, trying her best to dodge the showers. She was in an electric store perusing some TVs when she got a text from Mags.

'A wee favour, doll, I'm in town and running late. Can you call into the Withy Ale House and see Danny at the back bar? He has something Graeme needs for work for next week. If you fire it through our letterbox it would be brill. Let me know if okay, Thx Hun'.

The Withy Ale House was about a five-minute walk away, so not an issue, she told Mags she would leave it over in half an hour or so. When Sarah picked up the package from Danny, she thought she recognised him but wasn't exactly sure. What she was sure about, though, was how he could do with some manners or common courtesy - he barely spoke a word and muttered incoherently for the duration of the interaction, brief as it was. She thought she may have seen him at St Mark's, but on second thoughts, he didn't look the type to be hanging on Father Des' words on a Sunday, as entertaining as he could be. Nonetheless, she duly delivered her item at Mags and, seeing no lights on, dandered back to her digs.

Sarah had a lazy Saturday night in. Adam and Chloe were out for the night, and she had a nice relaxing evening watching some meaningless but entertaining telly. She dozed off on the sofa just after midnight and not long after this made it to bed. Not just in a deep sleep, she got a text from Mags at 12.34.

'Hey doll, guess where we are - your fav place Conty Club lol - missing a great night – a few going back to mines for a party if you fancy?'

Sarah just laughed and appreciated the thought but was more than content where she was and sent a brief reply, *'not tonight lol – enjoy Mags.'*

On Sunday morning at about 11.30, as fresh as a daisy once again, Sarah went over a bit early to St Mark's just in case Anne and Yvonne needed help getting set up. She passed the meeting room, as it was called, where she had started her Art classes. It was 'only' a beginners class, and Sarah was much more than a novice but still went along as they felt it was great to be once again in a 'creative space'. She was busy serving the meals when she got a call from Alex. Alex wasn't out with Mags last night, but no doubt was going to bring her up to speed on the antics from last night back at their house. She phoned again, but Sarah let it ring as she was busy-busy. She saw a text coming in but would get back to Alex in a bit as there were more pressing matters; the salivating Sunday punters were waiting.

Just as well she went over early as Father Des was unwell, meaning the girls were indeed extra busy. However, as ever, they had a good time and a bit later than normal just after 2 p.m. Anne locked up and all left for home.

Sarah then remembered her text from Alex and opened it.

'S - call me call me. Mags in hospital in A & E, its' bad'.

Sarah was in deep shock. What had happened to her? It must have been an accident. She called Alex right back, but there was no reply. She waited a few seconds, then called again—no answer. She waited a few seconds, then called again—no reply.

What could she do? Her heart was racing, she could get a taxi over to the hospital, she'd be there in five minutes, so she phoned and booked one straight away. She tried Mags - her phone was dead. This wasn't good. Her taxi was to be there in two minutes. Sarah waited, two-three-four-five-six minutes and no sign. Now in hysterics, she rang the taxi company back. Hang on, and it would be there in a minute, Despatch dismissively told Sarah. Four minutes later, the taxi arrived, and she was in A & E in a flash.

She went up to the receptionist and explained about Mags, but to Sarah's surprise, the receptionist assertively told her that unless she was direct family, under no circumstances would she divulge information about a patient. Sarah pleaded and pleaded, but the answer was still a categoric 'No'. Sarah, not sensing the queue forming behind her, in her desperation for news, wasn't picking up on the ire now building in the receptionist. Sarah was then told in no uncertain terms to leave. What next? She scoured the wider A & E area two or three times, but no sign of Mags, Alex, or Graeme, for that matter. She had only seen photos of him but felt she would recognise him if she had seen him.

She rang Alex. Again, no reply. Where next? Sarah was out of ideas and had no one else to ring. She glanced back at the A & E Receptionist and thought she would change her mind and go to the main reception. Nothing - Nada, no more information there.

What was she to do? Her mind boggled as to what could have happened. It must have been a car accident. Maybe she was taking Graeme back home to his place after staying over. She needed to do something…but maybe she had got ahead of herself here, maybe she wasn't so bad, had been discharged and was back at home sipping a coffee on her sofa. It was a twenty-five-thirty-minute walk to Mags' house, and on a mild enough day, she briskly made her way there.

As she arrived, she saw Mags' car there, untouched, a good sign, she thought. Alex didn't drive, so this was the only car in their yard. The other tenant had moved out before Christmas, so only Mags and Alex were there at the moment. However, there were no lights on and not much stirring as she rang the doorbell-once, twice, three times frantically.

Nothing or no one was moving, and Sarah was now bereft of ideas. She sat on the front doorstep for a few seconds in a daze, which turned into a few minutes. It was now starting to get dark, so she thought she better get back to her own house. There was nothing else to do here, and she could try Alex again when back there.

She was going to call Frances but decided not to; there was probably nothing she could do to help anyway. She made it back home. She was alone. She was helpless.

As she entered, she said a very quick hello to Adam but went straight to her room. She sat up on her bed and waited for Alex or maybe even Mags to call back. Finally, an hour after she returned home, Alex rang.

'Alex, is she alright, is she alright? Has she any broken bones?' … 'Calm down Sarah, calm down please…no, no, there's no broken bones'.

Alex went on to tell Sarah the full story. Alex came back from her own night out about 2-ish, and Mags, Graeme, and a few others were already partying. Sarah knew that the girls smoked the odd joint or two…but was unaware that Mags and Graeme, usually when in the company of Graeme's mates, would dabble in drugs a bit more sinister. Sarah, in her sheer innocence, hadn't picked up on this, despite Alex hinting a few times that Graeme was bad news. On Saturday night, Alex had smoked a joint, but the rest were on much stronger concoctions, and after some time with the party in full swing, Mags had fainted and was rushed to hospital. She had overdosed. Alex didn't know any more detail than this.

The last few weeks 'cooped up' had resulted in Mags going for it big time on Saturday night. Mags was 'blue-lighted' to A & E and taken straight to Intensive Care, which is why Sarah could not see sight or hear them when there. Mags remained there and was in a coma. The next 48 hours were crucial and would tell the tale. She had a good chance of recovery, but it would be two to three days before they would know more for sure. Alex had stayed at the hospital until an aunt living in Leeds, her designated next of kin, made it over. The aunt, Myra, rather than thanking Alex for staying, told Alex that she was not to have anything to do with Mags or any of her friends ever again. Wow! A bit much, Alex thought. Alex then told Sarah she needed to go - she needed to get her head down and get some sleep.

Sarah just about absorbed all of this…but what made it worse was that there was nothing she could do. She couldn't even visit poor Mags, hold her hand, or do anything else. She curled up in a ball in her bed and cried and cried and cried.

In no time it was midnight, but it would be a restless night for Sarah, she barely slept. She somehow summoned the energy to go into work on Monday. She said nothing to anyone, after all Mags did miss the odd Monday so it wasn't exactly breaking news. As promised Alex texted an update at lunchtime. There was no change but, in these situations, not a bad thing.

As she walked home from work, she got a call from Alex. Again, no change. Alex couldn't go to Intensive Care, as the family had warned her, but her insiders there had thankfully updated her. No change was maybe good news. Sarah made it to her bedroom, and then it hit her out of the blue, like a juggernaut!

The high-end 'gear' Mags got over the weekend was her; it was Sarah who got it to Mags. It had to have been the parcel she picked up from the Withy Ale House earlier in the afternoon. How could she have been so naïve, innocent, and bloody stupid? She was complicit in all of this. Why did she not stop to question what this was? This wasn't for Graeme's work it was for the party on Saturday night. She went straight to her bed, foetal position again.

Another restless evening, night and early morning. Sarah couldn't sleep. Bizarrely, she went for a walkabout at midnight to no avail. Come 7.30 a.m., she was still tired;

her head was in a spin. She was in no shape to go to work physically or mentally; by now, the brown paper bag was firmly etched in her mind. Mags was already out, and it may not look good if she was sick, too, given a permanent contact was in the pipeline, but Sarah couldn't garner the strength. She left a message with Nick and said she wouldn't be in as unwell. She went back to bed and finally got some sleep.

Chapter 13

Guilt

Later that day, she rang Alex for another update. No reply. She rang again, but No Reply. This wasn't helping. She thought she might walk over to the hospital but decided against it.

Alex called back soon after and updated Sarah. There was still no change, which again, according to Alex, was promising as she felt things had settled a bit. Sarah hadn't got it in her right now to tell Alex that she felt it was her who provided the drugs. She would do this later, she thought, but now was not the time. Another poor night's sleep ensued as the guilt engulfing Sarah meant she couldn't face work on the Wednesday either....... Guilt can be cruel, and there was no guilt like Catholic guilt; it riddled Sarah's body like a carcinogenic tumour.

She didn't know where to turn, out of embarrassment she couldn't contact Frances or Rosie. On the Wednesday morning, she decided to go over to St Mark's, settle her head and see if Father Des was about. Father Des, as expected tried to reassure Sarah that these things ...unfortunately do happen and she should dismiss the idea that it was her parcel that did the damage. 12.43 p.m. while with Father Des, the text came in from Alex.

'Mags is gone - passed away. complications, organ failure I'm told. I can't cope. call u later. RIP Mags beautiful soul'

Sarah stared at the text and stared again and again. She then tried calling Alex to no avail. She then held on to Father Des as close as she could for what seemed forever. He wisely said nothing let her empty her emotions and tears. A few minutes passed; Sarah regained her composure. Father Des invited her in for tea and when they had finished, told her he would call on her later that evening. He was true to his word, and boy, did Sarah need the company; her mind was racing. When he arrived, Adam pointed him to Sarah's bedroom. Sarah was in the depths of mourning and guilt. Mourning for the gift to the world that was the wacky and wonderful Mags McKechnie, who was no more. Was it the small brown parcel that proved the catalyst for her death, the truth was she might never find out. This was eating her up.

Alex called her later that night just as Father Des was about to leave. Sarah hugged Father Des tight, very tight, before he left. All she could garner from Alex was that there would be a post-mortem, but as soon as this was over, the body would be taken back to Glasgow for burial. The Intensive Care nursing team were instructed by the family that they did not want any of her Manchester friends to come to the funeral. Sarah felt this wasn't fair, and if she spoke to the family and explained who she was…they would surely make an exception. Wisely, Father Des put her off her notion. She so wanted to go and pay her respects but had to let it go.

On the work front, Sarah, as much as she had enjoyed the Health Authority, simply could not go back, not without Mags. At the end of the day, it was only a 'temp' job, so I'm not really losing out on that much. The downside to this would only hit Sarah in a few days. While out sick as a 'temp', she wouldn't be getting paid. She knew she would need to find other work and sharpish, but her head wasn't there yet. It wasn't helped by a text from Alex, who apologised to Sarah, saying she needed to clear her head and was going back to the North-East for a while. Sarah could understand this, but when she tried to call or text over the next few days, there was no response. A day or two later, the phone went dead. Alex had disappeared.

Father Des proved to be her saving grace at this point. She would spend the next few days helping out over at St Mark's, which helped give her a focus. After the initial shock and mourning, Father Des acutely knew what was at the route of her angst, Sarah believing she was a factor directly or indirectly in Mag's death. He saw her angst eat away at her with each passing day. She became more and more withdrawn and couldn't eat a full meal which wasn't helping matters either.

All of a sudden, it was 'rent day', and Sarah didn't have the full rent. She had blanked this from her mind, but the harsh reality had now set in. Frances could help but she didn't want to ask. She thought she would go to the bank and get a small loan - just enough to tide her over for a month or two. She couldn't believe it when they said they would have to consider her application and come back next week. Time was not on Sarah's side. In a panic, she rang the landlord and asked if her deposit would cover her rent for the next month. To which she was told bluntly, 'No…You don't pay then you're out', was the curt message back. The Landlord stressed how he had done her a massive favour and had a string of people who would take the room in a heartbeat. Things were at rock bottom - what was she going to do…where could she stay? In a fit of panic, she thought she could get the key to the large hall at St. Mark's from Anne, get a copy made and kip there if it came to it. She had even worked out the perfect excuse to ring Anne for the key.

Sarah had three days left to get money to the landlord. She simply couldn't face going to Frances but if she didn't, she was on the street. She had often heard the saying that you are only two or three paycheques away from being homeless and thought how stupid this was; this was now her harsh reality. Her life was in a mess, some hope of going to university next year - another pipedream!

She needed to get back to work asap, and despite not really feeling up to it, the next day, she made it into town to visit the same Recruitment Agency as before. While waiting to speak to the lady there, she got a call from Father Des. Father Des told her that there was no point being a priest unless he made use of the many contacts he had, and, on this occasion, it was the local police. They had often exchanged favours on the 'qt', for a nod and a wink - 'quid pro quo' so to speak. He told Sarah the Police had told him that the brown packet was still in Mags' house and untouched, meaning she had nothing to do with Mags' death. Sarah was relieved, so relieved it felt as if the Himalayas had been lifted from her shoulders.

This was brilliant news, and only on hearing this did Sarah feel alive again, but she still had the problem of rent money. Poor Sarah, the trials and tribulations of her life far removed from sleepy Ballycastle on the North Coast of Ireland now more than ever half a world away.

By now Father Des once again, almost as if he was on speed-dial to the man above sensed Sarah was struggling financially and offered to put her up in the Parochial House for a period if ever needed. She was after all practically working there so for once didn't feel guilty and glad too of the company but asked him not to mention anything to Frances. The next day she got an interview and landed another 'temp' role back in the city centre. Some light on the horizon at last.

The next afternoon, out of the blue, no idea how they even knew she was at St. Mark's, Darren and Ian Collins came from work to see how she was. She was really glad to see them and glad of their company. Darren had always reminded her of Lee, just a nice, cool bloke. The three spent well over an hour talking. It was great for Sarah, cathartic almost and helped her close this chapter in her life, her time at the Health Authority. She had many great memories there, most of course were courtesy of Mags. Gone but never forgotten. When they left, Sarah embraced Darren, and he quickly responded in kind. It was a nice moment.

She wasn't overly enamoured about her next role but knew she needed to get back on her feet again. Father Des sure proved to be her saviour alright - in more ways than she knew, but maybe not in the eyes of God. The reason being that he hadn't actually made a call to the police about the infamous brown packet…he felt with all that was going on, a small 'white lie' to unburden a tortured soul would surely do no harm. Sarah was thankfully none the wiser; sure, a priest would never lie! On the back of it, though, she was slowly but surely able to piece her life back together again.

It was indeed a new chapter and a new era for Sarah, and she'd have to roll with it. However, on the Sunday night before she was to start her new job, despite feeling much better, she began to regress. The thought of going into an office similar to her first one on the Oldham Road where there was constant bickering filled her with dread. She felt herself getting anxious. As much as she needed the money, she just couldn't do it.

She felt like going down to see Father Des, her new confidante and mentor, but thought she had bestowed enough worries on him of late. She would text the lady from the Agency right now and tell her the news. Back to square one. Sarah was in a proper bind. What to do? Where would she stay?

Then, from nowhere, a brainwave. Where was that number? She knew she had it somewhere. A few seconds later, she fumbled in her handbag and fumbled again before picking up the scrap of paper hidden away in one of the side pockets and dialled the number.

Chapter 14

New Era - New England

'Hello, Tony, Uncle Tony, is that you? It's Sarah here.... your niece Sarah'.

Within a couple of days, Tony had organised and paid for her ticket to Boston. Sarah felt she needed a new scene, somewhere to escape the ghosts of the recent past. A new continent would do the trick. It was only a few weeks ago that her and Tony discussed the idea of Sarah going to Boston, little did Sarah know it would happen at all, let alone so soon.

By mid-February it was still cold in Boston, Tony though assured Sarah the weather would pick up soon and she'd have a 'blast' and could stay as long as she liked. The security of a job with nearby accommodation included was a no-brainer and a great comfort blanket for her.

Tony heard the whole story about Mags; lock stock and barrel and told Sarah to chill out, take a few days to get to know the city and start work the next weekend. She has the choice between the bar or restaurant. She flicked a coin, the restaurant it would be.

Things would be quiet enough for a few weeks before the busy summer season started. This gives Sarah time to acclimatise. Not surprisingly, Tony was a very popular boss and as it turned out a fair one, respected by everyone who worked there. He had high standards which filtered down to his managers and all his staff. Sarah had no issues with this.

She got to know those in the house; it was a house Tony kept for those who worked in either the bar or restaurant. They were mostly in their twenties and early thirties and from all over the globe. Raul from Brazil was a Chef and hilarious, Stefan from Sweden his right-hand man. They were a bit older, nice people, interesting people and yes, a bit mad. A couple of the younger barmaids stayed there too but kept mainly to themselves but still good company just when Sarah needed it.

Sarah was due to start her first shift on the Friday evening but in her normal zeal and zest, asked if she could come in on the Thursday night and help out just to get a feel for things. She didn't want to get paid for this. Lenny Jackson, a local, the long-standing supervisor, was surprised but told her to go ahead, 'knock yourself out, kid', he proclaimed. Lenny and her as the weeks went on, would get on like a house on fire. Sarah was always on time, early in fact and had no problem staying behind to tidy up when needed. The ever-astute Tony was watching from afar, impressed but also proud of his niece. Tony and Sarah had really bonded, and she felt comfortable there. Right place, right time.

Slowly but surely, she found her feet in her new environment. By Easter things were busy which suited Sarah just fine. The busier she was the better she felt, always remaining calm and composed in a busy restaurant was a rare trait. Maybe Tony was right, she could make a career in hospitality there. Tips were good although with a communal policy for tips, they were evenly shared.

As much as she was settling into her own American dream, thoughts of what to do in the longer term were never far from her mind. She had consulted with Rosie as to a career move and was now fixed on going to university and finishing her education. She had good A-Levels behind her, but there was no guarantee she would get accepted as, technically, she was a 'mature' student. She liked the north of England and felt going back to Belfast would be too parochial for her. She applied to Leeds, Liverpool and Newcastle. Course-wise, it was a mix of English/Arts subjects or straight Teaching, which one she preferred, but she still wasn't exactly sure. She would have to do telephone interviews for all three which she was dreading. Thinking back to her first job interview in Manchester and the debacle it was…she only hoped these would be easier.

Sarah despite being a bit reserved, was naturally polite and engaging with all her customers. She was beginning to get to know some of the regular guests and enjoyed meeting them and hearing their backstories. On one Friday afternoon, a group of well-dressed middle-aged men came in and had a meal.

Even though Boston was the most Irish of all American cities, the locals there still loved the authentic Irish accent.

Someone from the northern tip of Ireland had their own distinct dialect and accent. As Sarah took the order, the head of the table was curious about her accent as she didn't initially place it. Hers was a bit different to the softer accent of middle Ireland. As the afternoon passed, she discussed with Scott, her new friend at the head of the table all things Art. Scott was an art aficionado and wasn't expecting a waitress in the local restaurant to be as well-informed as he was. Truth was Sarah was more knowledgeable than her guest. When he paid the cheque, he left a $50 dollar tip. Surprised, Sarah ran after him as he must have made a mistake, but no.

'Here that's for you, Sarah…go buy yourself a good Monet print'.

Claude Monet, the father of impressionism, was their favourite artist, and due to that common bond, Sarah received the biggest tip of her new career. Sarah was surprised and embarrassed all in one. This was almost as much as she would earn in her afternoon shift. As it transpired, he was head of a local legal firm and had come into the restaurant for the first time. impressed by the service and intellectual conversation, he would soon become a regular. Welcome to Uncle Sam, Sarah! Sarah was the talk of her colleagues all night, as they too would cash in on the 'tip'. It was not lost on Lenny or Uncle Tony either.

The bar was a decent size and a typical 'Irish' bar. Memories of the 'old country' were festooned in every nook and cranny. Pride of place, and behind the main bar was a massive portrait of JFK and a black and white 'signpost' for

Ballycastle. Sarah was blossoming in the role and maybe the more discerning clientele in the restaurant was the best place for her. Her confidence was now fully restored, and she was back to loving life. So much so that she was hoping cousin Rosie would come out for the summer. She begged and begged, but Rosie had a new boyfriend, and it just wasn't going to happen. A pity as she knew Rosie would have a ball out here.

Weeks flew in, and in no time, it was the start of the summer, and things were getting even busier. Sarah helped out in the bar now and again, as it could get a bit raucous at times, but the 'craic' was always good in there. The summer season always seen a few Irish based students come out to play Gaelic (Irish) football for the summer. The younger barmaids are waiting on bated breath to see the new talent on show and not necessarily their football talent.

The sun was shining most days, and there was a great atmosphere around the bar - what was not to like? Even though Sarah was not a sports fan, Tony had sponsored one of the local teams. By dint of this, the lads would always come into the bar after the games to celebrate or commiserate, result-dependent. By all accounts, they took their training and matches seriously but also enjoyed a good night out. On a Sunday after the game, songs would get going long into the night. It was an unwritten rule the footballers didn't have to work on a Monday. They were given jobs by local businessmen for the summer, often manual work, but Sunday was party night and Monday was recovery day. Sarah surprised herself and started going to and enjoying some of the games.

As she sat down to watch one of the games on a sun-bleached Sunday afternoon, she checked her phone and saw a text from a strange number with the text itself being somewhat strange also.

'Hiya - been a while I know but really need to chat to you - something I need to tell u - it's important. give me a call x'.

Sarah looked at the text, this didn't make much sense ….it was from a UK number alright …initially she thought she would call right back but suddenly she felt a bit uneasy about it all. Who was this? …Who could it possibly be? As she absorbed the text and let it sink in, she then thought maybe it was just a wrong number - if it was important, they would contact her again, surely?...as it turned out they would contact again.

Boyfriends were few and far between, and Sarah was still a bit guarded regarding the opposite sex. She had a snog with a couple of lads in the various city centre bars she would go to on a night off, but nothing too serious. It wasn't due to a lack of offers, though. These were 'ten a penny' given her job. However, there was one of the Irish lads she had a distant eye on. Working only occasionally in the bar, she didn't get to know the regulars as well as the others but, by now, knew most of the punters to see at least. There was one lad that caught her eye, Peter Doyle. Big Pete was from Galway, and he was just 'yummy' thought Sarah. He was tall, athletic, shaved blonde hair and was very, very handsome. He was the star midfielder on the team, and maybe this was the reason Sarah's interest in football grew. She'd keep an eye out for him, alright.

With the restaurant now at peak season Lenny needed a charge-hand, a supervisor of sorts under him and Sarah was the obvious choice. Lenny had remarked how good she was with the new summer staff, how patient she was while training them. Sarah gladly accepted, embracing the extra responsibility with gusto. The extra money would do no harm and help supplement her meagre student grant if she managed to make it to university.

One Thursday evening, when working in the bar, Pete came in with his usual side-kick, Frankie. Frankie was a bit louder, a typical Belfast boy, she thought. He wasn't shy on the banter stakes and, in no time, was flirting with Sarah and any of the other barmaids who would take him on. Her eyes were not on Frankie. Surreptitiously as ever, Sarah made a few discreet enquiries about Pete over the next few days. Bad news. Big Pete's girlfriend was coming out to join him for the latter part of the summer. Not good.

The next day almost as if to offset this setback, Sarah got an unexpected but welcome email. She was going to have a visitor. Someone coming out for a long weekend, and a male visitor at that. She was a bit surprised by the mail at first but thought, why not - let him come out and stay, see what happens. It would only be for a few days sure, and it would be strictly platonic. Now single, Manchester's very own John Travolta was coming to town.

Sarah had taken little or no days off, so Lenny gladly gave her the next weekend off so she could show him around town. Uncle Tony was very interested in the 'beau' as he thought it was…but was told by Sarah - it was just a friend. That said, Sarah couldn't wait until he arrived. She was the dutiful host and showed him around the sights and sounds of Boston. They had a great time. Was it still platonic, though? Time would tell.

Initially, yes, but his first two nights on the sofa turned into them reconvening to Sarah's bed. However, full-flung intercourse - the final step of her secular journey, although increasingly tempting was not just on the menu yet for Sarah. Well, until his last night - the inevitable happened and giving into temptation, Sarah was now a woman of the world. Of course, this was bound to happen at some stage in her new life, but although she really liked and trusted Darren, it was still a bit strange. Like her 'snog' with Gary back at the 'Conty Club', it was also a tad clumsy, but surprisingly, although reflective about it for sure, she didn't feel guilty.

The few days had passed in a heartbeat. They were getting on well, very well. It was now only a few weeks before Sarah would be returning to England to study. The summer sunshine of Boston was amazing, but she knew it would be a different story come winter. If she had any remaining doubts about returning to England, after last weekend, they were gone.

Sarah then arranged with Frances that she would stay with her for two-three weeks in September before university starting if it all went to plan. For 'uni', she was eagerly awaiting word back after her series of interviews.

Frustratingly, they were taking their time in coming back to her and she thought about ringing the colleges but decided to ride it out. Newcastle were first to come back, no good, rejected. She only hoped this was not a portent of things to come. It started to dawn on Sarah she had no plan B to 'Uni', this was her one and only cunning plan.

Sarah and Uncle Tony were still getting on great too which helped. Not as headstrong as her father, he had definitely found *his* vocation in life, in sunny New England.

One Thursday evening, when she was in the bar for a quiet drink and not too many about, she saw Pete Doyle come in and sit by himself. Very unlike Sarah, still intrigued by the shy lad from Galway, she sat down and introduced herself. He knew her to see, of course, and maybe because he was 'taken', she didn't feel anxious or nervous speaking to him. They had a nice conversation for about fifteen minutes as he waited on his mate, Frankie. This was a sure sign of her increasing confidence. Frankie had been out the summer before and, by all accounts, was fairly popular and likeable. Sarah still found him a bit loud and was surprised that he didn't drink. Frankie soon arrived and sat beside them.

'What's this, Doyler, you chatting up other women? I need to tell the beautiful one all about all of this'.

Pete just laughed and said, 'I'm not sure you know of this one, but this is our Frankie from Belfast'. You'll hear him before you see him…but to be fair, he has a great left peg'.

A great left peg indeed, Frankie along with Pete was the fulcrum of Tony's team. Pete, the engine room in midfield,

Frankie the wizard and playmaker up front, as well as chief scorer. Sarah as little else happening, sat on in their company for the rest of the night and enjoyed their chit-chat. Pete was studying medicine in Dublin with Frankie over in Liverpool doing a sports degree. As the night progressed, she found both to be good company.

Frankie was definitely the more gregarious, but beyond all the bluster, he seemed a decent lad, too. She enjoyed their company, their yin and yang, and it wouldn't be the only time she sat with them on a Thursday evening as the summer progressed. Even Frankie was growing on her.

On the university front, Sarah was by now as anxious as she was frustrated at not hearing any more updates.

She feared the worst when the following day, within an hour of each other, both came back to her and offered her a place. She spoke to a few close friends and family about which to choose. She also had a good conversation with her sister Mairead, whom she hadn't spoken to in a while. By now, Mairead had started her teaching career and loved it. Mainly due to this and the fact that she could do Art as well as English in Teacher Training, this had clinched the deal and no better place than Liverpool to study. Even though she didn't have an Art A-Level, her impressive portfolio ensured this wouldn't be an issue. As she spent the last couple of weeks in Boston, she was really content with her career choice, and the thought of rekindling the embryonic relationship that had started on the Boston sofa meant that back in 'Blighty', she had a lot to look forward to. She would soon be saying her goodbyes and definitely keeping in touch with Lenny and the dynamic duo of Raul and Stefan.

Tony insisted on driving Sarah to the airport, and as they embraced and said goodbye, he handed her a cheque for $1,000.00. Sarah looked up, aghast. She knew he could afford this but said she wouldn't be taking it. Her dad's obstinance was kicking in once again. Tony told her to go and enjoy herself at 'uni' and make sure and come back next year. He told her that this wasn't even half the profits he had made from Scott and his teams' now weekly trip to the restaurant, and there was only one person responsible for that.

'Take it, Sarah, this is how Uncle Sam rocks, you deserve it…see you next summer'. Sarah took the cheque, looked at it again, kissed her uncle, kissed the cheque in jest and ran to the check-in desk. As she joined the long queue, she checked her phone and saw a text; it was from the same number as two or three weeks ago.

'Hi - give me a quick call please, its urgent - x'.

Again, Sarah quickly dismissed it as a wrong number and prepared herself for the journey home.

Another student heading for the UK was sitting next to Sarah on the plane. A PhD student from Madrid who proved to be good company for Sarah. As they chit-chatted away, Sarah remembered the phone message she had from Maria Fernandez. Maria Fernandez had finally left a message a while back, which Sarah had ignored as preoccupied with more pressing matters. However, she had received another similar message a few weeks back, which she had saved this time but as yet hadn't bothered to return. Maybe her new best pal Lucia could translate it for her? That she soon did, leaving Sarah a bit perplexed. Lucia clarified it was indeed Santander, and that Maria worked in their Mortgage Department in Marbella. Lucia went on to say that as this was a private mortgage, Maria was bound by confidentiality, so they couldn't discuss the matter any further.

What, what was this all about? A mortgage, a private mortgage? This wasn't making much sense.

Then, the penny dropped! The special Euro account was for the Mother Superior, whom Sarah was never to touch or get involved with. This must have been for a mortgage in Marbella, Spain. Then there were Sister Benedict's frequent holidays - could the old biddy have been using convent funds to pay for her 'holiday home' and in none other than lavish Marbella, home of the rich and famous. Sarah shook her head, then smiled. 'Well, if you're going to do it, do it in style', she thought. This must have been why she erupted when she couldn't find the scrap of paper that day. The 'dirty dog' as Fran Delargy would say - no flies on old Bendy. For a minute or two, the thought of calling the convent and speaking to the Mother Superior crossed her mind - this would be the sweetest of all revenge missions…. but no, that was all in her past and probably best to leave it there. Sarah had a new and exciting life to look forward to. However, she couldn't wait to tell Frances on her return…she had to tell someone: Miss Marple, eat your heart out!

Chapter 15

A New Calling

Back with Frances and Lee, it was as if nothing had changed. Her small single bed was still intact. Frances was still blethering away harmlessly. Sometimes, Lee listened, and sometimes, he didn't bother. She had found a gem in Lee.

She thought of poor wee Mags - what a character she was, what an impression she made on Sarah. Sarah vowed that when she got herself settled, she would make a trip to Glasgow and visit her grave. A bit of a pilgrimage, leaving a few flowers, even doing a painting for her, it was the least she could do. For Sarah, although Mags had passed to her eternal rest, to Sarah, her soul and memory would live forever.

Sarah had told Frances about Darren coming out for a few days over the summer as he had broken up with Carly. Frances was a bit surprised but didn't comment further other than saying he seemed like a genuine lad.

She then told Frances about Bendy and the Marbella escapade. Frances couldn't believe it, for once rendering her speechless. After how she had treated Sarah, Frances was adamant Sarah should contact the convent immediately. Sarah wasn't so sure…but did say that she would think about it …but would she do it? Time will Tell.

At the weekend, she met up with Darren, had a few drinks and revisited the 'Conty' Club for old times' sake. On Sunday, she had a great catch-up and a laugh with the girls at St Mark's. Father Des was there too and delighted to see Sarah in such great form; this was reciprocated, of course. Sarah was a mere shell of a person when he last saw her. He felt she had grown up in so many ways, a quiet, confident air about her now. Sarah skipped off, thankfully still oblivious to his 'white lie'.

She had hoped to meet up with Darren during the week, but it didn't materialise as he was busy. She was enjoying the downtime after a busy summer and getting herself ready for college life.

On her last weekend with Frances, she met Darren in town on Friday night. This time, Darren treated her to a nice meal and some Italian wine, the wine this time in moderation. All seemed to be going well—they arranged to meet the next afternoon for a coffee, again in the city centre, as Darren lived on the other side of town.

However, the next day, as soon as Darren joined Sarah, she knew something was up. She quizzed him straight away, her intuition antennae never far wrong. Even before they got going properly as a couple, Darren wanted to break up.

Sarah was shocked, didn't see this coming. New to all of this, she thought she should at least listen to his reasons. He said he also had been through a lot recently, and with

Sarah going to be based in Liverpool, it wouldn't work. Too many complications. Sarah was struggling to compute it all, nothing adding up. Then, in a split second, she just got up and left, not saying a word. He shouted to her and muttered another apology, but Sarah was gone in a flash.

She went to the bus stop and tried to process all of this but couldn't work it out.

By the time she reached Withington, she had it all sussed. The lovely Carly must have been back on the scene. She laughed to herself for a second. After all…she had been through more challenging times this year. Another life lesson learned. She knew it wasn't exactly infatuation with Darren but would have been keen to explore things further. Carly didn't deserve him …but that was his choice.

When she got home, she told Frances. Frances, her usual diplomatic self, simply said, 'Do you know what, Sarah? You're heading off to 'uni'. Let me tell you, there's plenty more fish in the sea.'

As Sarah reflected, maybe it was for the best, Liverpool did sound exciting after all.

The following day, Sarah went into town to treat herself and spent some of Tony's money - well, it was her money, really. This perked her up, and some shorter skirts and tops were purchased. On her return, she told Frances she would cook for her and Lee the next night, her last before she headed for the beat around the Mersey. She was no Gordon Ramsey, but she made a decent effort. Yes, the fire alarm got tested a couple of times, but she eventually served up a decent meal…Sea food, of course. Her culinary skills were no doubt enhanced by her recent exploits in New England.

The next morning, Sarah packed her bags and made her way to Piccadilly train station. It was a while since she had been there. On the way there, her mood was dented for a split second when a middle-aged man all suited and booted bumped right into her. 'Excuse me,' she shouted and shouted at him she did! For a brief moment, Sarah thought to herself, 'Oh My God, what have I done here?' however, the man, obviously in a hurry, just shouted back, 'So sorry, Luv'. She was more than relieved he was so apologetic and in no way aggressive. She had even surprised herself with the reaction she had just unleashed. She afforded herself a wry smile.

As she saw the sign for Piccadilly-a flashback-she thought, 'Would the man selling papers still be there?' She smiled to herself again. After all, he was her first angel of the north.

<hr>

4th October 2012

So, exactly one year to the day when she had her flight of fancy from the convent, Sarah had made it to university. She felt proud as she entered the grounds for her registration for the first time. That night, in the Wellington bar after the convent exit, she wondered where she would be in a year's time; now she knew. If only Sister Bendy could see her now!

And…it was almost three years to the day since she entered the convent as a naive but enthusiastic girl. She was now a woman in her own right. Yes, Darren was a bit of a setback, but as she contemplated her thoughts from a year ago, she was sure that finally, three years later and via a more circuitous route than the average student, she had found her true vocation - Teaching. She strolled towards registration as if walking on air - and who knows, she might even bump into the affable Frankie from Belfast. After all, she would hear him before she would see him.

Then, just as she made her way along the busy, narrow concourse, her phone beeped. She had a text, the same number as before, but this time, they had put their name to it—a blast from the past.

'Sarah - sorry it's been a while I know - but would be good to meet up, there's something I need to tell you - the police have been in touch and they need to speak to you urgently - chat soon I hope, Luv Alex xx - p.s. forgot to leave my name before soz'.

This surely was a bolt from the blue! Momentarily, Sarah was stunned. As she stopped in her tracks and made sense of the message, she thought, 'Why now?' Why after all this time? In her mind, Sarah had moved on from all of this, and her first thoughts were to ignore it…but then the image of the 'brown bag' flashed into her mind. Jesus, what to do?

Then, the now more confident Sarah without much further thought, said to herself, 'Feck it', if they wanted to get in touch they can come and find her. She replied to the text, *'Sorry but I don't know a Sarah - Tony'.* That was it, time to blank it from her mind and concentrate on student life and some much-needed partying. Much deserved she thought after her working sojourn in Boston.

Sarah made her way towards Registration, but as it was early, she grabbed a coffee and sat down, watching the world go by. Then her phone rang again. It was a different number, so she thought she would answer it this time.

'This is Detective Inspector Muntari from Greater Manchester Police, I'm looking to speak to Sarah Delargy'. Sarah instantly panicked and shut down the call.

'Jesus', she said to herself. Her head was in a spin; she didn't know what to do. She took a couple of deep breaths and looked around to see if anyone had noticed her. Not a sinner was looking at her. Good.

With her heart still racing, she saw a message left on her phone from the same number. She knew this time around she could not dismiss or ignore it. She took another couple of long, deep breaths and listened back to the message.

'Sorry, we seemed to get cut off there. This is Detective Inspector Emmanuel Muntari from Greater Manchester Police. I'm from the fraud team and we would like to speak to you as soon as possible. We believe you were recently attached to one of the Carmelite convents in London. It's just so you know we have arrested an elderly female from the convent on suspicion of a mortgage fraud and we would like you to help us with our enquires. So, and just so you're clear here ... you are not under investigation in any way, simply contacting you to help us with our ongoing enquiries. Please call me anytime on this number, Ta'.

What the hell? Time for another deep breath. To say Sarah was relieved this was why the Police were trying to make contact was an understatement. Her initial shock turned to bewilderment…then and only then, she afforded herself a smile and a shake of the head.

In the last twelve months, Sarah Delargy had encountered her fair share of trials and tribulations - but this was the 'daddy of them all'. It was Bendy…but would she go to prison? Time will tell!

Her mind then meandered back to words from Sister Angela a while back. She shook her head and smiled again, 'Sarah, you know I'm a big believer in Karma, things will work themselves out, trust me'.

About the Author

Niall (Barney) Conway is a published author and part-time Playwright and enjoys all forms of creative writing. Although living in Belfast, he comes from Dunamanagh village in North Tyrone originally and an ex-alumni of St Columb's College, Derry.

www.ingramcontent.com/pod-product-compliance
Lightning Source LLC
Chambersburg PA
CBHW030027200726
48283CB00014B/2713